Double Down

By
Desiree Holt

Copyright © 2017 by Desiree Holt
ISBN: 978-1-68361-151-6
Cover art by Ravenborn Covers

Published by
Decadent Publishing Company, LLC

Look for us online at:
www.decadentpublishing.com

~A Note from the Author~

People ask me all the time if I always wanted to be a writer. I don't know if "always" is the word but certainly for all the years I can remember. I was a voracious reads, as were my mother and sister and books held a royal place in our home. The funny thing is I always thought I would write mysteries because that's what we all read. I didn't read my first romance until 2004, when I was sitting with the same three chapters of a mystery on my computer that had been there for three months. But then my eyes were opened and they never closed.

Submitting that first book was scary, but after a lot of rejections you stop being scared and become determined I'm glad I never gave up, because I am having the most fun in my life I have ever had. (Well, maybe not *ever!* LOL!) So here I am, with all these titles under my belt.

Writing a book is a solitary experience but it never comes to the bookshelves, virtual or other, alone. For me it starts my treasured friend and beta reader extraordinaire, Margie Hager, who has the best eagle eye in the world. Thank you, Margie my love, for all the hours you put in to help me bring my stories to life. And for your friendship, which is a highlight of my life. And to Janet Rodman who always looks out for me.

Then there is my family. Do they read my books? Absolutely not! But they are the best public relations team in the world. From my daughter Amy who tells all her clients about me to my son Steve who makes sure he lets everyone he knows when I have a book released to my younger daughter Suzanne who is my good right hand and my granddaughter Kayla who is my wonderful left hand. Guys, I could not do it without you. If you see me at a convention, Suzanne will not be far from my side.

My cats, of course, keep me company while I write. And you all have seen pictures of Bast at the keyboard with me. She thinks she should get co-author credit!
Thanks to all the people who let me pester them for information, on all the different topics I tackle, from SEALs to Force Recon Marines to Delta Force soldiers to the local sheriff to the people at Beretta and the folks at the San Antonio Stock Show and Rodeo. I'm sure I've forgotten someone and if I have, I am so sorry because the time you continue to give me is very special.

Last but very far from least, are all of you, my wonderful readers, who send me such great emails and posts and are so faithful. A special shoutout to Phuong Phen, Fedora Chen, Shirley Long and Patricia Sager who have been with me since my journey started and in frustrating times give me the inspiration to push ahead.

I love you so much. You are my extended family and I send you all many hugs.
There are a lot more stories to come. Please stay tuned.

I love to hear from my readers. You can write to me at *desireeholt@desireeholt.com* and I hope you will do that.

Where else can you find me?"
www.desireeholt.com
www.desireeholttellsall.com
Facebook: www.facebook.com/authordesireeholt
Twitter: @desireeholt
Pinterest: www.pinterest.com/desiree02holt

I look forward to hearing from all of you.

Desiree

Dedication

To Master Nate, Master Dan and The Lair in San Antonio, Texas, who made me understand the intricacies of BDSM and the emotion behind it.

Chapter One

Lee Sullivan detached herself from the group with whom she'd been chatting and moved with ease through the large gathering of people. The annual Colby, Inc. company picnic was in full swing. It was being held, as always, on corporate property, five prime acres north of the San Antonio city limits. Among other things, the site boasted a jogging track, a baseball diamond, and a park-like area with plenty of large oak trees, as well as an abundance of picnic tables and benches for outdoor lunches. Five years running, Colby, Inc. had won the award for best company to work for from the State of Texas.

As the mayor's chief public relations officer, she had a lot of high-profile events on her calendar, but the annual Colby, Inc. picnic had never been one of them. Until now. The mayor was angling for a major gift from the company to restore a park and playground.

"I need you to put in an appearance." Mayor Vincent had been firm about it. "I can't go because a major conflict in my schedule popped up literally overnight. I know I promised you a free weekend, but the possibility of a major grant from Colby, Inc. is too big to turn down." He shook his head. "I need you to represent me. You've done it before. You're good at it."

"I understand." And she did. All too well. Subbing for His Honor was becoming more and more a regular thing.

"Take Clay with you," he'd insisted. "Enjoy yourself."

Spending a couple of hours with Clay Porter, the city attorney, wouldn't be too bad. He was an acceptable escort, although not quite her type. She liked the challenge of the alpha male with the hidden submissive side. She had a feeling Clay would be no challenge at all. They were friends, as well, and often caught a late dinner or lunch together.

Oh, well, she'd told herself. *What's a few hours on a Sunday afternoon, anyway?*

At the center of a group gathered at one of the food stations was the poster boy for it all, Branch Colby, as relaxed as if he was sitting in his own den. His face was very familiar to her. She'd seen plenty of him in newspaper and magazine shots. On television. At parties for five hundred of his most intimate friends, usually with some over-the-top gorgeous female hanging on his arm. Seldom the same female twice. But all of his dates wore the same expression: look who I'm with tonight.

Today, however, was the first time she'd been close to him in an informal setting. In the flesh, so to speak. She had to admit it was awesome flesh. A soft-collared shirt embroidered with his company logo paired with what she was sure were very expensive jeans barely disguised the leashed power of the tall, well-muscled, well-tanned body. Thick brown hair shot with streaks of gold was razor-cut in short layers to make it lie smooth on his head and flat against his nape. His long legs looked as if they could run a marathon without halting.

He stood in a relaxed, loose-limbed pose, hands in his pockets, but, even in such a casual posture, everything about him said command. Authority. I'm in charge, his body language shouted. Definitely a man comfortable in his own skin, he looked like nothing less than a jungle predator waiting to pounce on its prey. Confident. Self-assured.

Arrogant!

He'd have to be, she thought, to own a company bearing just his name, nothing else to even identify the kind of business it was.

She'd read in *Texas Monthly* that he got his start working as a journeyman carpenter in construction, swinging a hammer and wielding a saw. He was a long way from his humble beginnings now, heading his own international land development firm. Every bit of what he had was built from that raw start, and he'd done it with sweat and savvy.

She watched the female guests, the married ones as well as the single, eye him with sexual avarice plain on their faces. Any one of them would give it all up for him if he crooked a finger, but she didn't see that as his style. Branch Colby was the real thing. No doubt about it.

She knew plenty of men like him. In fact, he reminded her of many of her favorite submissives, men who held positions of authority. In the seclusion of Infinity, the private dungeon where she had a membership, she had brought many of them to their

3

knees, quite literally. In the club, she was Mistress Star, a much sought-after Domme. These men bowed to her wishes without hesitation, aroused by the power shift and the excitement of giving over control to her. Of serving her.

She often caught some of these men on television or the news blogs, dressed in their custom suits and looking like the forceful titans they were. She'd smile, remembering them naked before her as they gave her pleasure, much as she gave it to them. Plenty of men at this picnic thought they were top of the heap—like Branch Colby. Some of them had even served as her sub at Infinity. There was nothing better than bringing out the inner sub in a powerful man, making him hers for one hour or one evening then watching him don his cloak of power as he stepped out of the club. Would Branch Colby ever agree to submit to her? She snorted. The entire polar ice cap would melt first.

Once someone had asked her if she worried that the truth about her sexual life would come out and affect her position with the mayor. She'd just grinned and shaken her head, knowing the men she played with would have to give up secrets of their own if they gave up hers.

If anything bothered her at all—and then only in the rare dark moments at night—it was the fact the excess of variety was beginning to wear thin. For the first time in her life, she wondered what it would be like to have a permanent situation, to bond with someone and create a life together. She had seen many others do it, but, until lately, she hadn't thought about it for herself.

Lee allowed herself a tiny smile as she watched

her host move with ease on to another group, different people, wearing his charm like a second skin. Sexual magnetism emanated from him like radio waves crackling in the air. It wasn't just his good looks or the way he carried himself. It was the whole package, made even more tempting because he wasn't throwing his power around the way some men did.

She worked the crowd as she'd learned to do, effortlessly, seamlessly, every point of contact casual and with ease, making sure to speak to the key people in attendance and pass along the mayor's greetings. Thanking his political supporters and giving them a few extra moments of her attention. Watching for her opportunity to introduce herself to Branch and tell him how sorry Mayor Vincent was he had to miss the picnic. No reporters, thank the lord. Branch had made it a point when he started these picnics that they not be fodder for reporters. This was a private affair in all aspects, and he had the security force in place to back up his mandate.

When she had completed her circuit of required contacts, she left Clay in an intense discussion with a member of the city council and wandered off past the fringes of the crowd. Time to give herself a little breathing room. She could watch her host from afar, admiring the man's air of absolute command. Did he ever let go of that tight control? A stray thought crept into her brain, and she wondered how he'd react to the demands of a Domme. Unbidden, an image flashed in her mind of the man naked and oiled and stretched out on a St. Andrew's cross, waiting for her attention.

Feeling a hot flush creeping up her cheeks, she

fetched a bottle of water from one of the bars set up at the perimeter and carried it to a nearby picnic table. As she lifted the bottle to her lips, she sensed a presence behind her.

"I must be doing something wrong. You can't be enjoying yourself too much if you're hiding over here under a tree all alone."

And there he was, as if her thoughts had conjured him up. His voice was like warm syrup, covering her with a thick layer of heat, and an unexpected tremor skittered over her spine. She looked up into eyes, so dark they were almost black, framed by the kind of thick lashes women would kill for. Tiny lines bracketed his mouth and eyes in a face the word rugged did scant justice to, all painted with a deep tan speaking of hours spent outdoors. She knew he spent as little time in his office as possible, insisting that, while he had a business, he was not a businessman. He ran the corporation from a high-end laptop and cell phone, preferring instead to visit projects and indulge in outdoor activities. It was apparent it worked, judging by his rating in Forbes.

She pulled out her political voice, friendly but cool.

"On the contrary, I'm doing fine. More than fine."

This was not a man you gave an opening to. She controlled the urge to check the clips holding her hair away from her face and smooth down her tailored blouse and thin cotton slacks. It wouldn't do to let this man think she had a personal interest in his opinion of her. She held out her hand.

"Lee Sullivan. I don't believe we've met before."

"I know I'd remember it if we had. Besides, I

don't think the mayor's spin doctor needs an introduction."

Tiny lines crinkled at his eyes as his mouth curved in that high-octane smile and his large hand enfolded her smaller one.

"Branch Colby."

The contact generated unexpected electricity. With practiced smoothness, she slipped her hand from his.

"And I think it would be hard not to know who you are, either, Mr. Colby."

"The cost of doing business, but it's Branch," he replied. "Please." One eyebrow lifted. "What's Lee short for?"

"Lee." She swallowed a smile. "What's Branch short for?"

He laughed. "Point to you."

"I didn't know we were keeping score." She looked up at him, into those dark eyes. "I should think you'd have guests a lot more important than me to spend your time with."

"You know, the funny thing is, they all seem to be doing fine without me." He swung in a lazy movement onto the bench opposite her, his posture relaxed. "I thought I'd come over and introduce myself."

Lee looked around to see if Clay was anywhere nearby.

"Your date is in earnest discussion with a member of the city council," he told her. "I wouldn't have thought Clay Porter was your type."

She quirked an eyebrow. "I didn't know I had a type. What would that be?"

He shrugged. "Forceful. Commanding. In

charge."

Maybe on the outside, like many of her subs who held positions of power. Yes, she liked a man who had great inner strength and power, but one who gave it up willingly in the dungeon or the bedroom. She'd come to realize part of the attraction was the contrast. She would never be happy with a man who was a submissive in all areas of his life.

"Clay is a very interesting person to be with," she told him. "We enjoy each other's company."

"You sound like you're describing an evening with my mother."

"Point to you," she said.

"This is the first one of these you've attended." He made it a statement, not a question.

She widened her eyes a fraction. "You can remember who attended each one with this mob scene?"

He winked. "Memory for people is part of my stock in trade. So what brought you today?'

"The mayor had an engagement he couldn't change, so we hoped you'd think I was an acceptable substitute."

"In that case, shouldn't you have found an opportunity to drag me aside some time during the day?" His dark eyes were unreadable. "Talk to me about the project he wants me to fund? Don't you want to tell me how important it is? What a great thing I'd be doing?"

She shrugged. "Not today. This is a social occasion. If I wanted to make a pitch, I'd be more apt to make an appointment with you to discuss it. Besides, it's obvious you know how important it is. "

"Would we be working together on this project

going forward?" he asked, those eyes still locked onto her like twin lasers.

Her pulse ratcheted up a notch, beating hard between her thighs, and heat flashed through her body. She lifted the water bottle and took a long swallow from it, hoping to cool her blood. She needed to be cool with this man, no doubt about it. He wasn't only about control. He'd *invented* it. She could imagine the battle their dominant wills would engage in.

Everything about Branch Colby screamed danger, but damn! The light brush of his hand against her sent shivers skittering along her spine and her heart rate escalating. If she could find a way to loosen that control, to have him on his knees, not just wanting her domination but craving it.

Dream on.

She had plenty of other powerful men to play with—except that wasn't quite what she wanted. Branch Colby would be a real challenge, although taking that challenge might be like walking into a fire.

She stared back at him, never breaking eye contact. She was good at that.

"Then you're planning to fund it? The mayor and the city council will be very happy."

Her boss would be doing the happy dance around his office.

"I'm on the verge of being persuaded." He stroked the tip of one finger over the back of her hand, nothing more than a quick touch.

Lee took her cell phone from her pants pocket and pulled up her reminder list. "Great. Let me arrange a meeting with His Honor to—"

"No." He touched her hand again, pressing it

down to the table. "I want to discuss it with you."

Her eyes widened. "Me?" Then she laughed. "That's very flattering, but I'm not sure my boss would appreciate being left out of this."

"He won't be. You'll report everything back to him. I'm sure you're up to speed on the details?"

More than she wanted to be. She'd read the damn proposal so much she had it memorized so she could brief the press and answer questions every time the topic came up. She was also very aware that Avery Vincent, good as he was at his job, had a raging need to be front and center on everything. Only a critical policy meeting had kept him from this picnic today, a venue where he would have taken every advantage to make himself known. Preened, if she was truthful.

"So?"

His voice shook her out of her mental wanderings.

"What will it be, Miss Public Relations?"

She frowned. "Are you making fun of me?"

"Not at all. I'm dead serious." His hand still rested over hers, pressing down on the cell.

She eased her hand away. No touching, she told herself. A tactile connection seemed to run between his fingers and her brain, and she didn't need that nude vision of him blasting back into her mind again.

"I'll have to clear it with the mayor."

Branch nodded. "Of course." He took her cell phone from her and programmed in a number. "When you get it cleared, give me a call. We'll set up a time."

He rose, took a long, hard look at her as if he could see clear inside her, then ambled away. In a moment, he had eased himself into a group of people who were only too glad to be gabbing with *the* Branch Colby.

Lee sat where she was, immobilized. What had happened here? They had introduced themselves and had a business conversation. Right? Yet the grass beneath her feet felt as if it had turned into quicksand.

***

Branch handed a drink to the man standing near him. Maximiliano "Max" Ferlita, his longtime best friend and attorney lowered himself into one of the deep armchairs in Branch's big office and stretched out his feet to rest on the ottoman. All the guests had left, and now the cleanup crew was doing its thing. Branch could have left, but he wasn't yet ready to head back to his house, which had for some strange reason become too large for him.

"Good turnout today," Max mused, sipping at the aged bourbon in his glass.

Branch nodded. "This is one of the few events I host I actually enjoy." He dropped into an armchair at an angle to Max's and took a sip of his own drink. "Although sometimes I wonder what it would be like to go to a party where no one knew who I was."

"Good luck with that. I'm not sure there's a place like that anymore." Max laughed. "You ever think about what it was like in the beginning for us?"

"You mean back when we scraped to have a nickel between us and had to scrape for everything?"

Max nodded. "Yeah. Back then. You were working construction, sweating your ass off in the summer and freezing it in the winter."

"And you"—Branch pointed at him—"were hacking it at a call center during the day and going to law school at night. How much fun was that?"

"About as much fun as what you were doing." Max studied him. "Did you ever, even for a minute, think we'd be where we are today?"

Branch took a long swallow of his drink and thought about what Max said. "No. Well, yeah. Maybe. When I was so dog tired I couldn't lift my arms and wondered why I wanted to get up and go to work the next day."

"Yeah, same for me." He grinned. "Then that construction company you were working for went bust and we had a chance to pick it up for pennies."

"Literally."

Max laughed. "That was all we had. I still don't know how we pulled it off."

"And yet here we are today, with Colby, Inc. and Ferlita Associates. A mega corporation and an international law firm. Two punks off the streets."

Max sobered. "I don't think I can thank you quite enough for giving me a piece of Colby, Inc."

"In the beginning, it was a piece of nothing," Branch recalled. "We've been lucky. Besides, you earn it every day keeping my ass legal and putting up barricades against the bloodsuckers."

They raised their glasses in a silent toast and then drank.

"So." Max nodded at him over his drink. "I saw the mayor's publicity flack here today. His honor too tied up to make it?"

"I guarantee you, whatever conflict Vincent had he couldn't get out of. He never misses a chance to suck my dick."

"Personally, I'd rather have her doing it. Although that isn't quite her style."

Branch lifted an eyebrow. He had gotten no vibes from Lee Sullivan that she preferred women to men, and picking up vibes was something that was a talent of his..

"Are you telling me she bats for the other team?"

Max burst out laughing. "Far from it. You just hang out in the wrong places."

Now Branch was getting irritated. "Do you want to tell me what the hell you're talking about?"

"I guess you spend too much of your playtime at Ultra. Or your own bedroom." Max laughed again, as if enjoying some kind of secret joke. "Unlike me. I like variety."

"So you've visited Infinity. So what?"

Yeah, so what? One of the many things binding their friendship so tight was the fact that, after a friend had taken them to a public dungeon in their twenties, they had both realized they had strong Dom tendencies they needed to pursue. They soon found, if they wanted to play, they had to take instruction, and what an experience that had been.

"Enough of this shit." Branch leaned forward. "Whatever's on your mind, spit it out."

"You know how Ultra has its own celebrities, Doms and Dommes who everyone wants time with? Oh, wait." He snapped his fingers. "Aren't you one of them? Right! Master B. The subs line up for an hour of your time."

"You are pissing me off here, Max. What does this have to do with Lee Sullivan?"

"Infinity's got its own celebrities, too, which you'd know if you ever got a guest pass like I did."

"And?" Branch made a "come on" motion with his fingers.

"And I discovered when I visited there that the most in-demand Domme is Mistress Star." Max leaned forward, watching his friend with an intent stare. "Who in real life is known as Lee Sullivan."

Branch felt as if someone had taken a cattle prod to his balls. "Are you fucking kidding me?"

"Not a bit." It was obvious Max was enjoying the reaction. He got up and went to the bar to refresh his drink. "I was given to understand that male submissives sign up well in advance to spend time with her."

Branch frowned. "Was she there the night you were? Did she see you?"

"No." Max shook his head. "I was in the lounge, in a corner with some friends, when she came in before a session." He grinned. "She had a damn good-looking sub waiting for her. Anyway, I wanted to be sure I wasn't mistaken, so I asked the friend I was with."

"If it was her, you mean?"

"Uh huh. Because my friend knew I'd keep my mouth shut. Infinity is no different than Ultra. No one ever discusses anything outside those walls. Not who they saw or who did what with whom. You know very well there are people who live the lifestyle who make it known to anyone who asks them. Many of the couples even socialize outside the club, but you know the unwritten rule—what happens at the club stays at the club."

"I suppose it wouldn't do me any good to ask you to get me some details on her."

Max shook his head. "You know better than

that."

"Damn." Branch took another swallow of his drink. "I wonder if I should ask for a reciprocity pass for a couple of weeks."

"Does that mean you're going after her? Hell, Branch, you can have your pick of any woman you want."

He lifted a shoulder. "It's the ones who aren't so ripe for the plucking that appeal to me."

He sat back in his chair and idly shook his glass so the ice cubes tinkled. Lee Sullivan was a Domme? His cock hardened, and a slow ache generated in his balls. All kinds of images swirled in his mind. Lee in a corset, thigh-high boots with tall, skinny heels, hair a blonde cloud around her head, her lips painted a ruby red, and in her hand a coiled whip. Or handcuffs. Or a cock ring. Or—

He gave himself a mental shake. She didn't fit on his preferred menu, for sure. He liked his women spicy and inventive, but there was never any question about who was in control. It was always him. One hundred percent. As he thought about it, though, he felt a smile tease at his mouth. What a challenge it would be to bend her to his will. To make her submit. To—

"Whatever you're thinking about," Max said, sitting down again, "you can forget it. Not happening, I can promise you that."

"Everyone has a trigger," Branch pointed out. "You have to find it. That's all." He stared at his friend. "Out of curiosity, have you ever, you know...."

"Played with Mistress Star?" Max grinned at him. "I'm tempted to say yes just to yank your chain, but no. Submission isn't my style. Any more than it's yours, if I may say so."

"But I'll bet I can make it hers, though." Anticipation made his cock stir.

"It will never happen. No way." Max shook his head. "No. Fucking. Way."

"Yes, way. Are you saying I'm not up to the challenge?"

"Yeah, as a matter of fact, I am. No one is. She's a legend at Infinity."

"You want to make that bet official?" Branch asked.

Max frowned. "What did you have in mind?"

"One night. That's it. I get her to willingly submit to me for one night, and I win. Is it a bet?"

Max looked at him for a long time. "You know, one of these days one of your bets is going to get you into trouble."

Branch leaned back in his chair and eyed his friend. "You think so? I don't. Adds a little spice to my life."

Max frowned. "Do you hear yourself? Spice in your life? Betting on something like this? When did you get so jaded? Don't you think it's time to settle down? We aren't kids anymore, you know."

"You first," Branch told him.

Max gave him a quizzical look. "Don't you ever get tired of all the phonies hanging on your arm? Don't you ever want something a lot more?"

"I gave up expecting that a long time ago." He couldn't conceal the bitterness creeping into his voice. He knew without a doubt why the women he dated spent time with him. They used each other—he used them for sex and they used him for the high public profile that went along with being his companion. Not an honest emotion between them.

"Maybe that's what makes me different than you. I still think it's out there. I look for the connection, and you look for the challenge."

"Maybe that's what turns me on."

And that's the way Branch liked it. Neat and tidy, no messy emotions.

He hated to think Max was right. Jaded? Was he really? It was difficult to admit to himself Max might be right. And he hated to think he was turning into an object of criticism for his friend.

He didn't want to admit it, but Max's words hit a little too close to home. He'd spent all these years working his ass off and had built a business that had garnered him an international reputation. He was cautious in his relationships, aware his money and his power were very appealing to so many women. He'd learned long ago to guard his emotions to the point where now he wondered if he was meant to be single forever. Of late, however, he'd realized something vital was missing from his life. Something not even Ultra seemed to fill.

He wished he knew what.

He took another slug of his drink and tamped down his unpleasant thoughts.

"I'm fine, Max. Since when do you object to our little wagers, anyway?"

Max shrugged. "Maybe since I took a look at us and wondered if we've turned into overgrown frat boys. We both turned forty not too long ago. One of these days you'll meet a woman who pushes all your buttons. Then your little habit—okay, our little habit—is going to come back and haunt you."

For a moment, he was tempted to tell Max to

forget the whole thing, but he liked a challenge. And Lee Sullivan, so cool, so self-possessed, impressed him as just that.

"I think you're depressing me," he said. "Are you in or not?"

Max hesitated a moment then nodded. "In, but let's make it for something worthwhile because I'll enjoy scoring it off you."

Branch nodded. "You name it, then."

Max studied his ice cubes for a moment. "Okay. A hundred grand. Let's make it payable to the charity of the winner's choice. I'll feel better about it."

Branch thought for a moment. The money wasn't a lot to either of them, not these days. And they could do something worthwhile with it, so a bonus.

"You're on."

"We need a time limit, though," Max told him. "I don't plan to let you drag this out forever."

"Time limit." Branch nodded. "Fine. One month."

"You may need more than that," Max cautioned. "This is not going to be as easy as you think."

"Is that so? How about doubling down if I do it in less?" Branch teased.

"God, you are a cocky bastard. Okay, less than a month and we double down." Max chuckled. "I'll give you this. You've got balls if you think you can get Mistress Star on her knees inside of one month. I'll take that bet." He rubbed his hands. "And start looking to see where I think the money will do the most good."

Branch slugged down the rest of his drink. If Lee Sullivan didn't call him by Tuesday, he'd contact her. He planned to come out on top here. In more than one way.

Only—

Only why did he all of a sudden feel as if he might be making a huge mistake here?

Chapter Two

When Lee pulled into the parking lot at Infinity, she noticed how full it was for a weekday evening. She hoped one of her favorite submissives would be there. She'd been so antsy since the Colby picnic; she needed something to work off her excess sexual energy. Entering the building housing the club, she nodded to the tuxedoed bouncer at the door, smiled, and then headed for the changing room. Lockers lined one wall, and, across from them, individual cubicles gave members privacy while they morphed from their public self to their dungeon persona. Lee chose to dress at home except on very rare occasions, so she hung her long coat in one of the lockers along with her keys and the mini-purse she carried for makeup and money. In the women's vanity area, she took a last look in the mirror to make sure she was put together. Satisfied, she strode with confidence toward the main room of the club.

Almost every seat was taken at the small tables, the sofas, and the big chairs. The hum of conversation was muted as people spoke in low tones. Alcohol was not served at the club, but glasses of soft drinks or ice water sat on the low tables along with coffee cups.

"Good evening, Mistress."

John Francona, the owner of the club, was leaning against the curved half wall at the entrance to the lounge, dressed in his usual gray silk shirt and black silk slacks. Lee had always thought the man, with his long dark hair and hint of dark beard on his square jaw, looked like a modern version of The Shadow. He was, however, the most knowledgeable person she had ever met in the community, ran the club according to strict rules, and knew how to handle the members. He also kept the membership to what he believed a workable number, which meant there was always a waiting list.

She nodded at him now as she stood surveying the crowd. She noted some couples she was friendly with making a midweek visit. A few of them were in various stages of undress, a common occurrence at Infinity. Doms and Dommes often took the opportunity to show off their sub's assets, a silent acknowledgment of ownership and submission. Others were engaged in quiet conversation, maybe discussing the evening's opportunities.

Lee drew in a long breath and let it out in a slow stream. This was the moment when the electricity always buzzed through her body, making her nerve endings snap and her pulse kick into a staccato beat. The hunger for a naked male body, bent to her bidding, craving the pleasure of the pain she inflicted, made her mouth dry with sexual hunger.

She had spent a tense few days since the picnic, unable to wash the image of Branch Colby from her mind. And how exasperating was that? Even though there were alpha males who found sexual satisfaction as submissives, she would bet money he was not one of them. She could still see him as he'd been at the event, outlined by the sun like some golden god. Sun-shot hair cut close and lying perfectly on his nape, broad shoulders and flat abs defined by the soft material of his polo shirt, long legs encased in denim moving with a smooth step as he strode about the grounds. She could imagine women tracing every line of his body with their fingertips, caressing that tanned skin, running their fingers through his razor-cut hair. When he had sat down at the picnic table with her and rested his arms on the wood, she had seen the play of sculpted muscles in his arms. The impact of his presence had been like an actual physical touch to her body.

If she had been a different type of woman, another type of person sexually, she might want to see what he was like beneath the image he presented to the world. The problem with that was she had seen other couples who had this kind of attraction to each other, both Dominants, struggle to find a common ground. It almost always ended wrong. And so it would for her.. She had no inner sub craving to be released. She'd tested that before with disastrous results.

No, if she and Branch Colby moved beyond being business acquaintances, they would end up flaming out. She didn't need that. What she needed, tonight as a matter of fact, was one of her most alpha subs who battled her for control even as they gave it up to her. Always knowing that would be the end result, but making her work for it. Yes, that was the thing that would do her the most good.

"Busy for a weeknight."

One corner of John's mouth hitched in a half-smile. "Seems the membership has a lot of energy to work off on Hump Day." He chuckled. "If you'll pardon the pun. Should I assume that applies to you, also?"

Yes, it definitely does.

She'd been buzzed since the Colby picnic, almost as if she'd been drinking fine wine, yet every one of her senses was hyper alert. The worst part was, she refused to admit to herself why. Branch Colby had pushed her buttons, and tonight she needed a sub ready for a good workout. She looked over the room with a long, slow glance, taking in the people gathered there, looking to see if she might recognize someone who particularly appealed to her.

"Drew is here tonight." John nodded in the direction of a conversation group. "I didn't mention you'd called to reserve your usual room in case you had other intentions."

Lee shifted her gaze, and yes, there he was, her tall pro athlete with the white-blond hair and piercing blue eyes. Whoever would have thought such a macho specimen would crave the role of submissive? Yet, the first time she'd met him, talked to him, he had explained it was almost a relief for him to be able to bend to someone else's will for a change. Until he'd tried it the first time, he hadn't understood the enormous sexual satisfaction of serving a Mistress. Now he was a regular at Infinity, a place where everyone's identity was as well guarded as the gold at Fort Knox. One thing both members and guests could count on at this dungeon—the lack of idle gossip.

"Thank you." She smiled at John. "I believe I'll wander over that way."

As she approached the small group, Drew spotted her and rose at once to his feet. He wore a loose shirt and leather pants, the material soft and supple enough she could see the thick outline of his cock beneath it. His eyes lit up, although he kept his face impassive. Some who came here—she called them indiscriminate bottoms— would obey the wishes of any Mistress who plucked them for an evening's enjoyment. Not Drew, though. He was one of those special subs who lived to serve a very small selection of Mistresses. That made the satisfaction in their play so much more intense and enjoyable. Yes, he was just what she needed tonight.

"Hello, Drew. I'm pleased to see you here tonight."

"Good evening, Mistress." He bowed his head in a deferential gesture.

"Have you already made plans?"

She knew there were two other Dommes with whom he played on a regular basis. The three women respected each other's territory with him.

"No." He grinned, showing his gleaming white teeth. "As a matter of fact, I was hoping you would be here."

She quirked an eyebrow. "Any particular reason or just the usual?"

"I wanted to show you something. A surprise for you." He looked at the couple he'd been chatting with, and they grinned up at him. "I told Garth and Malia, but I wanted to wait to display it for your eyes."

"Well, don't keep me waiting," she commanded.

"Show your Mistress your surprise."

He tugged the hem of his shirt from his pants, letting it fall loose about his hips, and with slow, teasing deliberation unbuttoned each of the brass buttons holding the flimsy material together. When the last fastener had popped through the buttonhole, he pulled the fabric apart to expose his chest. Lee's eyes widened a fraction. The hard, muscled hairless chest was a familiar sight to her, but what was new were two small golden rings, one dangling from each nipple.

She licked her lower lip, slicking her tongue over the red lipstick. They had discussed this the last few times they had spent time together. She had a fascination with nipple rings for men, aware of the male sensitivity there, and she knew Drew's nipples would be even more responsive than usual with his piercings. With a slow movement of her finger she reached out one finger and gave a light tug on one of the rings, knowing the sensation would be like a streak of lightning to his cock and his balls. She would have used her teeth, her preference, but she would save that for when they were in a room alone.

Drew's nostrils flared just a fraction, and her own nipples tingled in response to his reaction.

"Very nice," she said at last. "A nice treat for your Mistress."

"Just for you," he acknowledged. "I can choose not to wear them for others if it pleases you."

"We'll see."

She smoothed a hand over the fly of his pants, feeling the hard bulge of his cock and then, beneath it, his balls. She gave his sac a gentle squeeze, then increased the pressure and was rewarded by the slight intake of his breath. She looked down at the couple he'd been sitting with.

"Thank you for keeping Drew company, but I'm sure you'll excuse us now."

"Of course." Malia gave her a knowing smile. "I hope you both enjoy your evening."

Lee turned and headed toward John, still at his post, well aware Drew would follow her. The owner smiled as she approached.

"I have your usual room reserved and ready for you, Mistress Star." He slid a small key card from his pocket and handed it to her. "I'm sure you'll both enjoy your evening."

Lee strode down the thick carpet of the hallway, Drew following her. She slid the key card into the lock of the room she always preferred. Inside, she turned and watched as Drew closed the door then came to stand before her, hands behind his back, but he had not bowed his head, instead giving her a direct look. Such a battle he fought each time, making her work for every degree of submission he gave her. She had come to realize, however, for him, half the need, half the satisfaction, was making her work for it. And hoping she would increase the punishment as she did so.

Tonight he would more than get what he wished for. She had her own demons to battle and a hunger that needed to be sated.

"Safe word, please," she reminded him, "before we proceed further."

"It is the same, Mistress."

She scowled at him. "Are you being insolent?"

"No, no, Mistress. Not at all." He cleared his throat. "Symphony."

Ah, yes. Because he saw the sexual play they engaged in as musical parts that all came together as one smooth piece at the end.

"Remove your clothes, insolent sub," she ordered. "Do not keep me waiting."

"Yes, Mistress."

But he did it with a deliberate insolence Anticipation blazed in his eyes as he undid the buttons on the cuffs and slid out of his shirt, folding it and placing it on a small table against the wall. Next came the shoes, loafers he toed off with no problem. No socks. He'd once told her he hated wearing them and avoided them at all costs. The leather pants were made of such thin fabric that, rather than the usual button and zipper, they were held together with narrow laces. He opened the placket slowly, his eyes still locked with hers, daring her to order him to move faster. Oh, yes, Drew was a sub driven by the need to challenge her.

That was why he never closed his eyes, even at the peak of pleasure and pain, even while a climax ripped through his body. Lee knew he needed that connection and used her eyes to control him as much as anything else.

When the slacks had been loosened, he eased them down his narrow hips and long legs, stepped out of them, and placed them on the table with his shirt. Returning to his former position, he stood with legs apart, hands clasped behind him, displaying his wares for her inspection. God, he had a magnificent cock. Long and thick, with a dark plum-colored head, it sprang free and pointed toward his flat abdomen. Beneath it, his testicles lay heavy in a sac against his thighs.

Not hurrying, she circled his body and took in every delicious inch of him. Broad shoulders tapered to narrow hips, his belly so hard and flat it made the cut of the pubic bone more obvious. His legs were long and muscular, with a light dusting of hair much darker than the blazing white on his head. Equally dark curls of hair formed a line from his navel straight to his penis, like a line drawn on a map. Sometimes she gave in to an urge to lick him all over, to use her mouth on every inch of him while he was forced to hold back his release.

What should be her choices tonight? She needed an orgasm with a desire that bordered on desperation, but she had no intention of having him thrust his shaft inside her. She reserved that for the ultimate reward after a night of complete and very satisfying BDSM play, a night when her submissive had satisfied her in many other ways and she permitted it as his reward.

She studied the room, although she was so familiar with its contents and layout she could have drawn it in her sleep. The walls were painted a soft cream, soothing, to counteract the whirlpool of emotions that would spin in its confines. Dark wood beams were spaced across the ceiling, a variety of manacles and other restraints attached to them, ready to be lowered at a moment's notice. The carpeting was as thick here as in the rest of Infinity, except for a large polished square of wood. Sometimes a Dominant wanted his or her submissive to kneel on the unforgiving surface of the wood rather than the soft cushioning of the carpet.

In one corner stood the St. Andrew's cross, made of dark gray wood and fastened together with gleaming metal strips and bolts. This was a favorite of hers when she used the flogger and the crop, although tonight it didn't fit what she had in mind. The spanking bench stood by itself, thickly padded with dark brown leather. Coiled on hooks along one side were wide leather straps for the times when restraining a sub was desired. She'd brought this particular sub to orgasm on that bench using a paddle many times. Tonight she wanted—needed—something different.

She stopped at the tilted board, a well-polished slab of honey-colored wood that was well padded and had rows of leather straps attached along both long sides. Yes, that would do very nicely.

Drew had not moved from his pose, awaiting her instructions, but she could almost see his body vibrating with the need for punishment and satisfaction.

"Go and stand by the board," she commanded.

He stared at her for a long moment, heat flaring in his eyes before he moved. Leaving him to wonder what she had planned, she opened the top drawer in the armoire against one wall and with deliberate care selected the items she'd need. Next she removed three things from the rack on the wall and carried everything to a table near the board. Drew's gaze shifted to take everything in, but he made no comment.

"I'm going to remove those nipple rings for a moment, sub. When I return them, there will be a little something extra added.

He stood silent and motionless while she detached the rings one at a time. Then she threaded first one then the other through a bead that had a tiny cylinder attached to it. When she had them both ready, she took one, threaded the needle-thin metal though the piercing on one nipple and locked it into place. Then she repeated the process with the other nipple. Picking up a fob from the little table, she depressed the button on it. The muscles in Drew's body tightened as the tiny vibrators attached to the nipple rings kicked into gear, sending tremors stimulating his nerve endings. She permitted herself a tiny smile of satisfaction at his reaction.

"I can alter the intensity," she informed him. "We'll leave it on low for the moment." She fiddled with the adjustments on the board until it was tilted at a forty-five degree angle then nodded at Drew. "You know what I'm looking for. Take your position against the board. And, Drew? Remember the rules. You do not come until I give you permission."

"Yes, Mistress." His voice had the rough sound of loose gravel, already tight with the effort at restraint.

He'd done it many times before. This was not a new game for them. Tonight she planned to add something, but that was for later. Without saying a word he leaned against the board, bracing his feet on the floor. Still, his eyes were trained on her. She knew it would take the entire playtime before he reached the point where he lowered his gaze in ultimate submission.

She seldom talked to her subs, except to give them instructions. She was not here for conversation. She had plenty of that in her job. So she kept silent as she applied scented oil from a tiny bottle to Drew's sculpted, magnificent muscles and body contours. Stroking his skin gave her inordinate pleasure, stimulating her senses and sparking her nerve endings. She caressed him, with a slow glide of her fingers, tracing every ridge and indentation.

When she reached his cock, she poured a tiny drop of the oil in her palm and wrapped her fingers around his swollen shaft. She took her time, caressing his cock up and down, her eyes focused on his face to watch his reaction. The slight intake of breath, the narrowing of his eyes, the twitch of muscle in his jaw were his only signs of response.

Lee was careful to keep her caresses at a gradual and steady pace. She wanted him aroused but not yet to the point of orgasm. No, that would be the ultimate release for him when she was finished. She noted the increased rise and fall of his chest as she worked the oil into his skin and the drumming of his pulse at the hollow of his throat. The more her fingers massaged the oil into his cock, the more his muscles tightened and his body tensed, every movement she made heightened by the tiny vibrations the enhanced nipple rings were sending through him. She loved to watch him fight off response, to hold back unless she commanded him otherwise. She heard the hissing intake of his breath when she rubbed the oil into the soft skin of his scrotum, taking a moment to manipulate his balls with her fingers.

When she finished, she capped the bottle and set it aside. Then, working with careful precision, she lifted each strap attached to the sides of the board and fastened them around Drew's body. Narrower straps wound around each leg and back to the edge of the board so the tongue of the buckle could pierce the hole of the leather. Then came the bindings for the arms so he was secured to the board, arms held down at his sides, unable to move. The final strap, wider than the others, crossed over his groin and fastened on the other side. He could move his head but little else. Early in their sessions, she had discovered the restraints alone aroused him, presenting him as 100 percent helpless and at her mercy. Which, indeed, he was.

Next, she selected three circles of flexible material, cock rings she slid with great care over his engorged penis. She found the use of these incredibly stimulating for her submissives, and Drew had almost exploded the first time she circled them around his penis. Fitting them tightly at the base of his shaft would cut off the regular flow of blood and cause his shaft to swell and thicken even more. She turned her head to catch his expression and saw heat blazing from his eyes, turning his irises electric blue. How easily he was aroused these days; how little punishment it took to push him to this point. Soon he might not present enough challenge to her, but for now? He was just what she needed.

Exhaling a breath, she picked up her favorite flogger made of tiny outer strips of heavy leather with the inner ones softer for a lighter sting. She had discovered that, for Drew, this particular toy, more than any other, stimulated his endorphins. She licked the tip of one finger and brushed it back and forth over the head of his shaft, barely touching him and noting the rush of color to his face. Then, with a dexterous twist of her wrist, she swept the toy back and forth over his body, beginning at his ankles, working her way along his thighs, over his flat stomach, up the hard wall of his chest, and then, still with the same unhurried stroke, back down again.

She avoided his cock until she had made the

circuit three more times, all the time watching his reaction.

"I'm not going to permit you to fuck me tonight," she told him in a controlled voice.

When he opened his mouth to protest, she reached between his thighs and squeezed his balls. His nostrils flared, and the vein in his neck throbbed, but he remained mute.

"Tonight you will suck my pussy until I come. If you have done a good job and satisfied me, then I will permit you to enjoy your own climax."

He looked as if he'd strangle her if she would just release his bindings, but he gave a brief, restricted nod of his head. She knew the low, continued humming of the vibrators on the nipple rings was heightening everything he felt.

In another moment she replaced the flogger she'd been using with the special flogger she preferred, one with four short straps that had been stiffened and had cuts in them so, when it struck flesh, it made tiny stings in several places. This was one of Drew's favorite forms of punishment, the multiple little bites on his skin so erotic to his body she had to take care not to go overboard or it would be almost impossible for him to hold back his release.

But she was an expert with this implement, so much so she had been asked to train other Doms and Dommes in its use. She had confidence born of long experience. Twisting her wrist, she applied the flogger along his legs, smiling as she saw the pattern of red marks appear on his skin. The oil made them that much more pronounced. Ankle to thigh and back again. Wrist to shoulder and back again. Then repeating, over and over, until Drew was panting, the rush of endorphins pushing him toward a climax.

Just as suddenly, she stopped and tossed the toy aside. By this time, between the vibrating nipple rings, the bindings, and the floggers, she knew Drew was near his breaking point. She placed herself square in front of him, leaned close to his face, and put her lips near his ear.

"Do you want to come, my handsome sub?"

"Yes, please." His voice grated. "Please, Mistress."

"Me, first," she told him.

Pressing a button built into the board, she set a motor to humming, and the board tilted backward so his head was downward at about a forty-five degree angle. Placing her hands on her hips, she straddled his head, her stiletto heels giving her the extra height she needed, and placed her cunt right over his mouth.

"Through my panties," she whispered. "Use that very talented tongue of yours, and you will be rewarded."

She sensed the vibrations of his body as he strained for self-control, but she knew he would not disappoint her. He had learned early on the punishment for being a disobedient sub.

Her eyes glued to his face, she watched as he placed his lips on her and ran his rough tongue through her slit, silken fabric and all. She had worn her clit ring tonight, and it bumped against his jaw, setting off tremors in her cunt. Without being instructed, he knew to take it in his teeth and tug on it. The pressure and touch set off a low throbbing in her inner walls, sensations that skittered through her body. He lapped at the new freshet of her liquid and sucked again, sometimes pressing harder, sometimes easing up on the pressure. They'd done this dance before, so he knew what it took to bring her to climax. Not too fast, but not too slow. Just the right tempo. Stroke, stroke, stroke. Up and down the lips of her cunt, rubbing over her now-inflamed clit, a gentle bite now and then, and pulling that hard bud into his mouth.

She was so wet, she could smell her own scent, but she wanted to prolong this as much as possible. Every muscle in Drew's entire body was taut, clenched, straining against the straps that restrained every inch of him. His cock had swelled even more, the skin darkened from the restricted blood flow. The head had deepened to purple, shiny with the drops of precum spilling from the slit. She was familiar enough with his body to know he was at the ragged edge of orgasm and exerting all his self-control to await her permission.

"Faster," she told him now. Then she pulled the teeny scrap of fabric on her mound to the side. "I want your tongue inside me, sub. Right now."

Obediently he thrust it deep, scraping her inner walls. She rocked on it, adjusting herself so her clit rode over his lips as he fucked her with his tongue. Her response was enhanced even more by the sight of him restrained from shoulders to ankle and able to use only his mouth to pleasure her. She thought to close her eyes but, instead, looked downward, seeing only Drew's chin and the flex of his muscles beneath as he worked his tongue faster and faster.

There! She was almost there. A little more. A little....

Spasms gripped her, shaking her body, the muscles of her inner walls clamping down on Drew's tongue as her cream flooded his mouth. With an effort of will borne of long training, she held herself in place over his face until the last of the tremors subsided. She took a moment to pull herself together before she moved back from her position. When she looked down again, she saw Drew's mouth glistening with her juices. When he slid his tongue out to lap every last drop, desire flashed through her again.

But she was through for the night, at least as far as her own body went. Now it was time to reward her sub for his performance.

She pressed the button to return the board to its upright position then adjusted it even more so Drew was now tilted upwards at a forty-five degree angle. In complete silence and with great care, she unwound the straps, one at a time, letting them hang for an Infinity employee to clean later. She left only the wide band around his midriff to hold him in place. With the same precision, she removed the cock rings one at a time, hearing the combination sigh and groan from her sub as the blood began to flow unrestricted again. The thick vein wrapped around his shaft pulsed.

"You have done well," she complimented him. "Now it's your turn to achieve satisfaction." A tiny smile played at her lips. "I'm guessing this won't take very long."

"It will take as long as my Mistress wishes," he told her in a strangled voice.

"A very noble sentiment, but I think you have earned your release." She nudged a small footstool over and lowered herself to it. "I think tonight I would like to watch you bring yourself relief. I want to see that strong hand and narrow fingers stroke that cock until your cum spills over them onto your flesh. Begin now."

She stared in fascination as he gripped his penis, stroking at first at an unhurried pace then increasing the speed of his motion. She did not expect it to take long, especially since she had left the nipple rings in place, the vibrators attached to them on a very low hum. And she was right. In less than a minute, his cock pulsed, and semen spilled from the slit to run in thick rivulets over the back of his fingers. She gave a brief glance at his face and saw it tense with concentration. His breathing was ragged and irregular, and she saw the heavy beat of his pulse at his neck, a sure sign his heartbeat was rocketing.

When the aftershocks subsided, his big body relaxed, his muscles no longer straining, his breathing steadier. Completed at last, he lifted his hand and with great deliberation licked every drop of his cum from his skin. His eyes gleamed as he focused them on her, never wavering until he had captured the last bit of fluid.

Lee smiled at him. "Well done, sub. Very well done."

She rose from the stool, walked to his side, and bent her head. She ran her tongue over his lips in a slow sweep, licking the remnants of her taste and capturing a tiny bit of his essence with it. He smiled at her, flashing his white teeth.

"Thank you, Mistress Star."

"You earned it," she reminded him.

She busied herself releasing the last wide strap and then easing out the nipple rings. She removed the tiny vibrators and set them aside before cleaning his entire body of the oil with wet wipes. The last thing she did was wipe down the rings and insert them with great care back into the holes pierced for them, being very gentle with the tender tissue. Before she allowed him to move from the board, she fetched a bottle of water from the tiny fridge in one corner of the room and waited while he drank at least half of it. Then she held out her hand, although she knew he did not need her support. He had not gone as deep into subspace as she'd taken him many times, so his recovery time would be faster.

She watched the flex of the tight muscles of his buttocks as he strode over to where he had placed his clothes. The entire time he dressed he never looked away from her. When he finished, he stood for a moment, head bowed.

"Thank you for tonight, Mistress Star. I hope I pleased you."

She laughed. "You always please me, Drew, even though I sometimes feel you keep one last little piece of yourself apart. But we'll work on that."

He raised his head and looked for a moment as if he wanted to say something more.

"Yes?" she prompted. "Was there anything else?"

"Forgive me for my insolence, Mistress, but tonight I had the feeling you were not, well, committed to our playtime."

She studied his face for a moment and then his eyes, which she had a feeling saw far too much.

"I'm fine, Drew. Perhaps it was just a very tiring week." She grinned. "I'll let you distract me more thoroughly next time."

"Of course."

But later, as she drove home through the dark streets, she wondered if Drew might not be too perceptive. Despite her best efforts to concentrate on her sub tonight, he wasn't the one whose image flashed in her mind and kept intruding on her thoughts. Far from it. Every time she looked at Drew's face, it was Branch Colby who teased at her and ramped up her arousal. Damn!

How had the man lodged himself so firmly in her head in such a short amount of time?

Chapter Three

Branch swiveled in his desk chair to look out the window behind him. The entire wall was floor-to-ceiling glass, giving him an outstanding view of downtown San Antonio, including the famous Riverwalk. The location was what had inspired him to buy the ancient building on the site, tear it down, and build this one, keeping the top two floors for Colby, Inc.

He'd waited out the first three days of the workweek, doing his best to keep from checking his cell every five minutes in case he'd missed a call or a text. Not that he had a lot of time to sit around doing nothing. He was on the move a lot, visiting projects in process, some of them in other states, and that required taking his private plane. He had new project proposals to study, reports from his site manager to check out, and myriad other tasks that for the most part kept his brain 100 percent occupied.

But not this week. Instead, his brain was filled with images of a tall woman with a thick head of sable hair, mysterious hazel eyes, delicate cheekbones, and a mouth that begged to be kissed. By him, if he was honest enough to admit it. The casual clothing she'd worn to the picnic did little to disguise a body he wanted nothing more than to get his hands on. Long legs he could imagine wrapped around his waist. Slender shoulders. High, firm breasts and a rounded ass he itched to spank, turning the flesh a warm shade of red.

When Max had finally gone home the other night, Branch had stayed in his office a long time, driving himself nuts reliving his brief conversation with Lee Sullivan. He couldn't remember the last time a woman had gotten to him this way. What in hell was it about her, anyway? Maybe it was her cool but pleasant manner. Or it could be the fact that since she'd joined the mayor's staff and first landed on his horizon he didn't remember ever hearing about her hooked up with anyone. Not that he involved himself with gossip, but he made it his business to know who was doing what with whom. You never knew when you might need an edge with something.

Of course, the reason could be the bombshell Max had dropped on him. Mistress Star. A Domme, of all things. As a longtime Dom, Branch well knew the pleasures of BDSM play, the responses heightened by the combination of pleasure/pain, the power exchange between Master and sub when complete submission was achieved. But the women he partnered with craved that submission as part of their ultimate satisfaction. Lee didn't impress him as a woman who would submit easily, if at all.

And therein lay his problem. That dumbass stupid bet he'd made with Max. He couldn't even get the damn woman to give him a call, much less agree to submit to him in a D/s environment. And it irritated the hell out of him. Anyone else would have been on the phone to him at eight o'clock Monday morning.

But Lee Sullivan isn't most people.

That was the damn truth. And she pushed buttons he didn't even know he had.

Now it was Thursday morning, and he was done waiting. Point to Lee Sullivan for forcing him to make the next move, a strong signal she was as much about control as he was. Grinding his teeth, he asked Karen Jericho, his administrative assistant, to call Mayor Vincent's office and get his public relations officer on the line. Now.

"Tell her it's about the grant the mayor's been after me about," he added. "That should get her attention."

It rankled him he needed something to get her attention at all. He sat in his chair, feet up on the desk, fiddling with a stress ball shaped like a football while he waited for the connection to be made.

"Mr. Colby?" The voice came from the little speaker on his desk. "I have her on the line."

"Thanks. Put her through, please."

"Good morning." Her voice was like low, soft music, soothing to the nerves. With a voice that could hypnotize, it was no wonder she was so good at talking to the media, "To what do I owe this honor?"

"I thought you were going to call me."

He snapped the words out before he could think. Damn it. He was already putting himself at a disadvantage and maybe putting her on the defensive. He swallowed.

"Scratch that. I was hoping you would call."

A low chuckle reached through the wires. "Would

I be out of line if I suggested you're used to people doing exactly what you expect of them."

He answered with his own laugh. "You've got me there. Let's start over. Good morning, Miss Sullivan. Thank you for taking my call."

"You're more than welcome, Mr. Colby." He could hear the amusement in her voice. "To what do I owe the honor?"

"If you recall, I mentioned I'd like to discuss the mayor's request for a grant in further detail."

He wanted to make sure she knew there was a major benefit involved here. To control his edginess, he picked up a stray rubber band from his desk and hooked his fingers through it.

"And I suggested Mayor Vincent would be the optimum person to have that conversation with," she reminded him.

"Maybe so, but I'd rather discuss it with you."

He dropped his feet to the floor and sat forward in his chair. He wasn't above using a little blackmail to get what he wanted.

"Vincent has told me how important this project is to him. If he wants to move forward with it, then you and I are going to have a meeting."

She was silent for a long moment.

"Fine. I'm assuming you want me to come to your office? When would be a good time for you? I'm sure your schedule is far busier than mine."

He heard the touch of amusement again. Was she teasing him? Baiting him? He had become used to people bowing to his will and falling all over themselves to accommodate and please him. It was pleasant, for a change, to have someone challenge him.

"As a matter of fact," he told her, "I had something different in mind. Like dinner."

Again there was a silence.

"Fine. When were you hoping to do this? I'll need to check my calendar."

Little minx.

He laughed. "By all means. How does tonight look to you?"

"Tonight?"

"Yes." He stretched the rubber band. "Are you free?"

"I believe I'm available. Let me check."

He caught the difference in words and smiled. At last! A woman who it seemed wasn't impressed by him and who didn't mind tweaking him a little.

And a Domme. Remember that, idiot. And remember your stupid bet with Max.

"Mr. Colby? Did I lose you?"

He blinked. Had his mind wandered and taken a detour during this conversation? What the hell? And Mr. Colby? *Mister Colby?*

"Sorry. Someone brought something into my office. And it's Branch, please."

He had the uncomfortable feeling she was having a joke at his expense, a totally foreign experience to him these days.

"I asked you if seven thirty worked for you. I have late meetings, but that time is good."

"Seven thirty is fine." Eleven would be fine. Whatever time she said. "I'll pick you up a little before that."

"Not necessary. Tell me where, and I'll meet you there."

She damn well wasn't making this easy for him.

"Do you know where Chandler's is?"

He named a restaurant off the beaten path, in the northern suburb of San Antonio, one where he was least likely to run into people he knew. People who would interrupt their dinner. He would have no problem explaining dinner with a member of the mayor's staff, especially this member. He didn't want any distractions, though. He'd have invited her to his home if he thought she'd accept, but that was something he had to work up to.

"Yes, I'm familiar with it. I'll see you there at seven thirty."

Then she was gone, and he sat there, staring at the phone in his hand. He was still sitting there when the door to his office opened and Max strolled in.

"You look like a man who's just been asked an impossible question," Max joked.

"What?" He replaced the receiver. "Oh. No, no. Confirming a business meeting. Nothing more."

Max dropped into one of the big chairs in front of the desk. "Well, while you're having all your business meetings, I hope you aren't forgetting our little bet."

"Bet?" Branch raised an eyebrow.

Max threw back his head and laughed. "Nice try on the casual attitude, but I know you. That bet's been at the top of your mind since we made it. How's the progress coming in that area?"

"We said a month," Branch reminded him.

"Double down if it's less." His friend grinned. "Of course you could always pay me now, and we'll forget about the whole thing."

"Not on your life." He dropped the rubber band into a drawer. "You'll be the one paying up. I'm already making progress, if you must know."

Okay, so that was a little white lie. Or a big one.

Max's eyes lit up. "Yeah? Details, please."

"Uh-uh." Branch shook his head. "No advance info. Just be aware I have the situation under control."

"Is that a double entendre?"

"What?" Branch frowned. "No. Don't you have something to do? Can't you see I'm busy?"

"What I see is a man trying to find a way out of a quandary. But, okay, I'll let it rest for now. I came by to see if you wanted to catch dinner tonight."

And didn't that figure.

"Can't. I have a business dinner on the books."

"Then you must have made it five seconds ago because I checked your calendar with Karen."

Shit!

He fudged. "It came up less than an hour ago. I haven't told her yet."

"Okay, give me the info, and I'll tell her on my way out."

"I'll take care of it," Branch snapped. "Don't you have lawsuits to file or something?"

"I have a clear calendar." Max grinned at him again. "But since I can tell you're tied up"—he smirked—"I'll find a client to harass instead." He paused at the door. "Tell Lee Sullivan I said hello."

Branch resisted the urge to throw something at the door as it closed.

***

Lee nodded at the waiter who held her chair for her, settled into it, and looked across the table at Branch Colby. "I always enjoy this place. I've never had a bad meal here."

"Neither have I. They've got a great menu, too. No matter what you like, you can find it here."

"I agree."

She let her gaze drink in his appearance. He was 100 percent delicious male. There was no other word for it. And, when she inhaled, she caught the subtle hint of his pine-scented cologne even over the blend of aromas from the various foods being served. Looking at him, she got the same feeling she'd experienced at the picnic, almost a punch to the gut. There was something so electric about him, so erotically mesmerizing. And dark. She sensed a darkness in him that attracted her as much as anything else. But she wasn't so sure she wanted to explore it, either.

His business attire tonight contrasted with the casual clothes he'd worn at the picnic, but not less effective at accenting his appeal. His white shirt was in stark contrast to his tan, the dark brown of his tie and his business suit making the color of his eyes darken to onyx. She wondered if there was anything he wore that didn't make him appear mouthwateringly appealing. And then she wondered how he'd look with no clothes at all.

Her nipples contracted into painful points, and the pulse in her cunt set up an insistent throbbing.

Stop it!

The last person she should be entertaining erotic thoughts about was the man sitting across from her. She would bet a year's salary there wasn't one submissive drop in him. And, since she could say the same about herself, she could forget about any sexual overtones and get on with the business of the meeting. If only the air between them didn't crackle with unwanted electricity.

"I thought a bottle of wine would be nice. You okay with that?"

"Yes, please. That would be nice."

A glass of something white would no doubt ease her unexpected attack of nerves. This was nothing more than dinner, for god's sake. What was the matter with her?

He picked up the wine list the waiter had left.

"We ought to decide what to eat first so I'll know whether we need a red or a white."

"Oh. Well, you may be disappointed, but I can't drink red wine. Gives me migraines." She grimaced. "Annoys the hell out of people when I tell them that. I've heard every lecture possible about not pairing a white with any kind of meat."

He reached across the table and took one of her hands in his. "I personally think people should drink whatever they like. The hell with what their meal is."

"Wow. That's refreshing." With a casual movement she withdrew her hand from his. "I like a Riesling, but I'm open to anything."

Wait. Maybe she shouldn't have said that. Would he take it the wrong way? Why did she have to be so careful of everything she said to him, as if they were engaged in some kind of verbal game?

You know. Go ahead. Admit it.

She shoved the devil from her shoulder.

"Riesling it is." He closed the wine list and studied her.

The sharpness of his gaze made her acutely aware of the fit of her dress, the rise and fall of her breasts beneath the soft fabric, even the way she held her hands on the table. Although his posture appeared relaxed, he still made her think of a jungle animal, a panther perhaps, poised and ready to strike its prey. She did not intend for it to be her.

"Do I have a speck on my face?" She brushed a hand over her cheek. "Is my lipstick smudged?" She hoped not. She'd taken great care to check it before she got out of her car.

"No, not at all." His smile could have melted butter. "I was thinking how beautiful you are. I'll bet a portrait painter would have a field day with you."

Lee burst out laughing. "I'll say this for you. Your line is a lot different from the ones I'm used to."

His lips curved in an engaging grin. "Then I'd have to say you're hanging out with the wrong people."

She took a sip of water to settle herself and picked up her menu. "Why don't we order? Then we can get down to the discussion of the mayor's project."

To his credit, he nodded and picked up his own menu.

He sampled the wine when it arrived, gave it his approval, and the waiter filled their goblets. He lifted his and gestured to her.

"To a successful project."

"Absolutely." Except...why did she get the feeling they were talking about two different things?

Dinner turned out to be more pleasant than she'd expected. From the little time she'd spent with him Sunday and the tone of his invitation, she'd assumed she'd be fighting off ambiguities and insinuations all night. Instead, he'd been thoughtful, charming, but not to excess. He seemed, interested in her job, asking intelligent questions about it. It wasn't hard to see how women fell into his lap and businessmen stood in line to partner in deals with him.

"You like to solve puzzles, don't you?" she remarked.

"Puzzles?"

"Mmm hmm. I think that's what people are to you. Puzzles. You dissect them and put them back together."

He chuckled. "Is that what you think I'm doing here?"

"Isn't it?" She took a sip of her wine.

"I'm just interested in you. In what makes you tick."

"See?" she pointed out. "Puzzles."

Branch laughed. "Okay, maybe, but I really am interested."

Lee wondered if he intended to discuss the mayor's project or not, or that had been an excuse. Over coffee and dessert, however—crème brûlée for her, French apple pie for him—he asked her for details. She had gone over it so many times from its inception it was all etched into her brain, and she had no problem giving him the information he asked for. Her biggest problem was trying not to stare at the smooth flex of muscles in his jaw as he chewed and in his throat as he swallowed. Or his long graceful fingers as he lifted his coffee cup for intermittent sips. She could visualize them stroking a woman's breast or her ass. See his lips placing a trail of kisses on feminine skin.

What she couldn't see was him on his knees, which was indeed a real catch in any relationship they might have.

Relationship? Get real, Lee. You are so far out of his class. If anything, he's toying with you for his amusement.

But she didn't think so. She had pretty good instincts about people, and he didn't seem that shallow, that false. Even his air of assuredness was lacking the arrogance she saw in most of the men she knew in his class. Still....

"Are you this knowledgeable about all of Vincent's projects?"

She shrugged. "Most of them. The media wants every little detail about everything on his agenda, even what he eats for lunch. The best thing is to be fully prepared. That way you can't say something they misunderstand."

He took a last swallow of coffee and sat back in his chair. "Okay, I'm convinced."

She widened her eyes. "Convinced? About the project?"

He nodded. "I have the figures in my office. I want to go over them one more time with my chief project manager, but I'd say we're a go here."

Wow! She had to clamp down on her excitement, although she wanted to bounce in her chair. Avery Vincent had touted this project to everyone as a cornerstone of his term in office. It would be a capstone in South San Antonio, his gift so to speak to the residents of the barrio. A park, with playground equipment and picnic facilities, a place for families to gather in the evening and on the weekend.

"Is it solid enough I can tell my boss?" She wanted no mistakes or missteps here.

"Why don't you wait until tomorrow afternoon?

If you can get me on his schedule, I'd like to tell him myself. I kicked it around with some of my people, and we have a few ideas on how to expand on it."

"Expand?" She tilted her head. "But that will require additional funding. I'm not sure—"

"Trust me." He leaned forward, elbows on the table. "I'm pretty sure he'll be pleased. Go ahead and get me on his calendar, if you would."

"I can promise you that won't be a problem."

She sat quietly while he took care of the check, and then he rose and pulled back her chair for her. As they exited the restaurant, he kept his hand at the small of her back, warm against her body, the heat traveling through her as if he'd touched her with a match. He walked her to her car in the parking lot and waited while she got out her keys and unlocked the door. When she turned to face him, he was so close she would have had a hard time sliding a sheet of paper between them. For a long moment, his gaze scorched her, amber lights shining in the darkness of his eyes.

Then he took a step back.

"Thank you for meeting me."

How formal!

"No problem. I'll call you in the morning with a time for the mayor."

"Excellent. I look forward to it." He turned to walk away.

Lee swallowed the little drop of disappointment that caught in her throat. What had she expected? A date? Why would she want one anyway? This was a situation that could go nowhere. Period.

But then he called back to her.

"Seven o'clock Saturday night? And this time I'll

pick you up. No arguments."

She was so stunned she answered without thinking. "All right."

"You can give me your address when I see you tomorrow."

She might as well. A man like him would find it in a matter of minutes anyway. In fact, she wouldn't be surprised if he already had it.

She watched him walk away with his easy, loose-hipped gait and heard the blip-blip from his vehicle as he pressed the fob to unlock it. When the headlights came on, she saw he was parked in the next row over. Sitting in her car, she waited until he had pulled out of his space. She was somewhat startled to see him in a big SUV. Was this the car he drove to his projects? She had expected him to drive something sexy like a Porsche or a sleek, high-end BMW.

So much for stereotypes, she told herself.

She realized, when he didn't move any farther that he was doing the gentlemanly thing and waiting to make sure she left the lot without a problem. As she headed toward home, she mulled the evening over in her mind, turning over and over every word he'd said, every nuance, every intimation. He had been completely circumspect. And yet she had the feeling he had a core agenda and, more than that, it concerned her. She wasn't sure if she was anxious for the following day to get here or wishing she could push it back.

Branch Colby lit a fire under emotions she'd spent years keeping banked. After so many failed relationships, she'd given up on expecting to find the one. She didn't know if that person was even out there. What she did know was, after one evening, Branch Colby had managed to reach those emotions still hidden deep inside her and bringing them into the open with this man would be dangerous to her mental and emotional health. He wasn't a man who was after more than just the moment. She'd do well to remember that.

Okay, then. Tomorrow night she was heading for Infinity again. Before Saturday night she needed to work off this excess sexual energy that surged through her with unexpected power.

Chapter Four

Once again Branch was prowling his office, clock-watching, trying to keep himself busy and driving Karen over the top crazy.

"If you come out here one more time and ask me if I'm sure the mayor's office hasn't called," she told him, "I may have to borrow one of your guns and shoot you. I can't believe this thing with the mayor is so damn important to you."

"I'm a good citizen who supports my community," he growled.

"Yeah, right. So write them a check and get back to work. Lord, you look like a caged tiger that missed its last meal." She picked up a slim folder and handed it to him. "Here. Keep yourself occupied. This is the list of the latest files on the hospital project. There are items that need your input."

"Fine." He grabbed it from her hand. "I'll be in my office if I get—any calls."

She almost but not quite hid a smile. "Of course you will."

He settled behind his desk and opened the first file on his computer. Forcing himself to focus, he began to absorb the details. Discipline took over so he was astonished to note the time was ten thirty when Karen buzzed him to tell him the mayor's office was on the line. He hoped it was Lee and not Vincent's secretary. He took a moment to settle himself before he answered.

"Hello."

"Good morning." Her voice was as musical as he recalled from the night before. "Mayor Vincent wondered if you're free to join him for lunch."

"If you're going to be there, I am."

"Is that a condition of the meeting?" she asked.

He could hear the teasing edge to her voice.

"Let's say it is. Would that be a problem?"

"Not at all. The mayor has asked me to join you, anyway. I think he's already planning what he wants in the media release."

Branch grunted. "Sounds like him."

They settled on the time and place, and Branch hung up. Settling back in his chair, he let the images from the previous night dance through his mind. He wished Lee Sullivan didn't push all his buttons the way she did. Three hours with her at dinner hadn't changed his sense of her at all. Even if Max hadn't told him she was a Domme, he might have suspected her tendencies. She was most definitely a woman in control of her situation at all times. Getting past that would no doubt be more difficult than he'd first believed. He'd better be up to the task, or Max would not only be taking his money, he'd also be laughing his ass off.

Four hours later, he hadn't seen anything to change his mind. The meeting with Mayor Vincent had gone off as he planned. When he announced

Colby, Inc. in addition to paying for the project would do all the work as well as, constructing a playing field and bleachers for games between neighborhood teams, the mayor almost kissed him, and Lee began taking notes and asking who at his company she should coordinate the media release with. He hadn't wanted a press conference. Truth be told, he hadn't even run it by his staff yet. Thank god they were used to him tossing stuff like this at them. He hoped no one—Max in particular—could figure out that this largess had been inspired by his need to impress Lee Sullivan.

It was a lot of money to get on her good side and open a door for him, but what the hell? Money had long ago ceased to be a problem for him. He might as well use what he had. He'd woo her as he had other women, snare her in his web, and bend her to his will. He hoped when it was all over—and it would be; he wasn't in the market for anything permanent— they could still be at least friendly acquaintances.

The last person he wanted to have waiting for him when he returned to his office was Max.

"Have you given up working for a living in favor of stalking me?" he grumbled.

Max chuckled. "Thanks to you I don't have to work for a living unless I want to, but, no, I had a meeting in the building, so I thought I'd check on your progress. Which I'm going to guess isn't much, although you may have pulled the devil's tail."

"Yeah?" Branch picked up the miniature football and squeezed it rhythmically. "What makes you say that?"

"Mistress Star was at Infinity last night." He paused. "In fact she was the headliner in the performance area."

"Performance?"

A tiny sliver of heat worked its way through Branch's body. He had taken part in performance nights at Ultra himself and understood the extremes of play required to entertain the crowd.

"She's very much in demand for it, as a matter of fact. She was juiced last night. Put her sub through a lot of paces." He rubbed his jaw. "I tell you, she wore a pair of white latex pants laced up the back that showed the flex of every muscle in her fine ass. She was magnificent, Branch, in full control of her subs at all times."

"Subs?"

He lifted an eyebrow, but that wasn't the only thing in his body that reacted. Imagining Lee in her mistress outfit conducting her performance with two subs had his cock thickening and pressing against the fly of his dress slacks.

"Yes, two of them." Max grinned. "And very willing. She had an attendant oil their bodies so the light would reflect from them, although I understand she makes it a habit to oil her subs from head to toe before she begins playtime."

"And what type of games did she play with them?" He hoped his voice was casual.

"Wondering what she'll choose for you when she gets you on your knees for her?"

"Hah!" Branch barked the word. "Never happening. You know that." He wiggled his fingers. "Come on, give. I want to know what turns her on so I can turn it around on her when I get *her* on her knees for *me*."

"You should come and watch for yourself next

time. But I will say she uses very effective ball gags on her subs when she's performing, and she enjoys a variety of restraints. Cock rings attached by a thin strip of leather to collars are among those she prefers."

Max paused to take a swallow of his coffee. "Last night she added a little something extra to one of her subs, a strap running from the cock ring down to his balls and up through the cleft of his ass to attach to the back of his collar. Then she kicked it into high gear. It was very evident, even though they were unable to speak by the time she was through with them, that they would do anything for a climax."

"Jesus!" Branch shifted in his chair, his own balls reacting to the image and a throbbing pulse beating in the vein wrapped around his penis.

"I wouldn't want it for myself," Max continued, "but I can tell you there were a lot of Doms watching who were stimulated enough by it to get themselves off in the dark of the viewing area."

Branch had been tempted many times to do that himself when a performance had been so outrageously outstanding. He'd always managed to keep himself in control, even when the air around him filled with the scent of male release.

"Anyway...." Max set his now empty mug on a coaster on Branch's desk. "Thought I'd let you know you might have bitten off more than you can chew here."

"Forget that."

"No kidding?" Max cocked his head. "If you're so damn confident, maybe you'd like to double the bet."

"You've got it."

The words were out of his mouth before he had a

chance to think. Still, what could he lose? He was confident he'd come out on top. Literally.

His friend laughed. "I'll be happy to collect on your failure, my friend. You're on."

After Max left, Branch sat in his chair, staring out at the view below him but not in fact seeing it. He'd have to ramp up the game sooner than he'd planned. Saturday night's plans needed changing. If she went for it, he'd be halfway there. He was counting on her sensual nature and natural curiosity, as well as her extreme confidence to control things, to make her say yes.

This call he made to her cell phone. He didn't want it going through her system or his.

"Find you're going to be too busy to fit me in tomorrow night?" she asked when she answered, that same amused tone in her voice.

"On the contrary. I was wondering how adventurous you are."

"Adventurous? That sounds interesting. In what way?"

"I had planned to make dinner reservations at Bellissima, you know, that new Italian restaurant in Alamo Heights?"

"I understand reservations are impossible to get. Don't tell me even the fabulous Branch Colby doesn't have enough influence for that."

"On the contrary," he teased. "I have it under control. I just thought maybe we ought to do something a little different."

"Different?" The hesitation in her voice was obvious. "Like what?"

"I keep a small powerboat at the Canyon Lake Marina. The drive's less than an hour, so if I pick you up in the afternoon, we can get out on the lake before the sun sets."

A pause. He was getting used to her pauses as she chewed things over.

"Dinner on the boat," he added. "I wouldn't want you to think I'm trying to cheat you out of a meal."

She laughed, that low musical sound he was becoming addicted to, that turned him on as it vibrated across the connection.

"A sunset dinner on the water," he went on, wondering if there was a chance she was going to turn him down. She was cautious, this one. Nobody's plaything, for sure.

"And what time would we be getting back?" she asked.

Okay. Not until morning if he had his choice.

"Whenever you're ready to head back in. Your call."

More silence. Then....

"All right. What time should I be ready?"

Yes! Branch had to resist the urge to give a fist pump.

"Two thirty okay? That'll give us plenty of time to get there, get out of the marina, and find a place to drop anchor. That work for you?"

"I'll be ready," she assured him.

"Bring a bathing suit and a sweater," he added.

She laughed again. "That's an odd combination."

"The suit so you can lie out in the sun and the sweater because it gets cool in the evening."

"I'll be waiting."

Branch disconnected the call and sat there, a kaleidoscope of thoughts running through his brain. He'd seen Lee Sullivan—what—three times? He didn't know how it had happened, but in the blink of an eye, she'd become a different kind of challenge to him, one he wasn't sure he was comfortable with.

Chapter Five

At least a dozen times Lee was on the verge of calling Branch Colby and cancelling. She wasn't an idiot. He might think he was concealing it, but there was no mistaking the underlying sexual innuendo in his invitation. What she had to decide was if she was ready to entertain accepting it.

There was something so intriguing about him, something beyond the mere dynamic of the self-made millionaire. Even in the meeting with her boss, she'd caught that same hint of darkness, of core eroticism. She was sure he'd be incredible in bed, maybe even addictive. There were two problems with that, however.

She had discovered casual relationships outside Infinity didn't work for her. She hesitated to involve herself with a man who had not one submissive tendency. She'd become an expert at sensing it by now, especially with the alphas like Drew who were so in control in every other aspect of their lives. Some of them, again like Drew, battled that submissive need, but when they gave in to it at last, the rewards were so rich it only made the desires stronger.

The dynamics were so unbelievable and so difficult for people in the vanilla life to understand. Not that they had a real understanding about the D/s lifestyle anyway, but that was a major reason why she kept her private life just that. Private. As she grew older, she came to the conclusion, albeit with reluctance, that she might never find the sub she'd be picking out drapes with or shopping for a home with.

Still, she was happy with her life. And maybe a "side trip" with Branch Colby might not be so bad, as long as they both understood the rules.

But what if she'd misread his signals? What if she was reading more into his invitation than he meant?

Jesus, Lee. Is this your first date?

She gave herself a sharp mental smack. By the time the doorbell rang Saturday afternoon, she was through dithering and ready to let go and enjoy herself, whatever happened.

When she opened the door and Branch stood there in shorts and a T-shirt, she had all she could do not to drool. He was freshly shaven, and the scent of his aftershave tantalized her nostrils again. The breadth of his shoulders and the musculature of his arms and chest were even more defined than in the other clothing she'd seen him in. The sculpted muscles were just as evident in his strong legs, his calves, and the masculine thighs disappearing into the legs of the shorts.

Lee hoped she wasn't drooling. If only she could convince him of the sublime satisfaction of submission, but she knew how futile that would be. The desire was either there, or it wasn't. She swallowed a sigh and put on a smile.

"All set?" he asked.

"I am." She lifted her tote. "Bathing suit and sweater, as ordered."

He took it from her hands. "Then let's get to it."

The drive to Canyon Lake took close to an hour but was pleasant and easy, Branch asked her what her preference in music was, found a station on satellite radio, and kept it on low the whole way, so the music was a quiet hum in the background. Lee thought she was an expert at guiding the course of a conversation, but Branch Colby made it an art form. She started to tell him the story of her life, until she reminded herself what that story was.

When they arrived at the marina, he parked his SUV and led her along the dock to where his boat was berthed. Boat? She stopped and stared at it. Small powerboat? Lee had seen plenty of boats before. Businessmen in San Antonio had invited the mayor to small gatherings on their boats, and often her presence had been required. Those were small powerboats. This thing? Forty-eight feet if it was an inch.

"Problem?" Branch touched her elbow.

"You said a small powerboat. I'd hate to see what you think of as big."

He chuckled. "I'm glad I didn't take you to the biggest one."

"You have another one?" *Dummy.* Of course he did.

"I often entertain on the water. I need something to accommodate larger groups." One corner of his mouth quirked up in a smile. "Want to take that one instead?"

"Uh, no, thanks. This will be fine." She winked at

him. "Cozy."

His laugh was like a shimmer of warmth sliding over her. "Come on. Let's get on board."

He helped her up the ladder someone had put in place then followed.

"Let me show you around before we cast off."

Carrying her tote in one hand, the other at her elbow to guide her, he walked her around the deck, pointing out the best areas to sun, indicating where the wheelhouse was up four steps then urging her down a short flight of steps into the interior.

"Galley, salon, two cabins. Just your basic little powerboat."

She burst out laughing. "That's like saying the Ritz Carlton is just your basic hotel."

"Oh, I think the Ritz is a little bigger than this. Come on, Lee, relax. Pretend this is nothing more than a rowboat."

"I'll do my best."

He settled her in the guest cabin, suggested she change into her bathing suit, and said he'd see her on deck when she was ready. She did a quick change but took a moment to check herself out in the mirror. *Damn!* Her nipples were like two hard points against the soft fabric of the bra. Too bad there was no concealing that. And slim hope Branch wouldn't notice. He was a man who observed everything.

She adjusted the miniscule bottom that barely covered her mound and gave thanks for her recent waxing session. Her legs were smooth all the way up, no stray little curly hairs peeping out from the edges of the material. Okay, then. She pulled her hair back into a ponytail and grabbed her lotion and a beach towel. The engines were already rumbling, the boat vibrating by the time she climbed the short flight of stairs again.

She waved up at Branch, who sat relaxed in the cockpit, and spread her towel out on one of the lounge chairs. No matter what else happened, she'd get a good layer of tan accomplished.

***

Branch congratulated himself on his behavior all afternoon. The moment Lee had emerged in that teeny, tiny bikini he'd wanted to lay her down on the deck and fuck her brains out. Instead, he motored them out of the marina, out onto the water, and gave thanks for the smooth surface of Canyon Lake. He took a moment to bring up the iced margaritas he'd had stocked in the fridge and served them both drinks then dropped anchor away from the main traffic and stretched out beside Lee Sullivan's very tempting body.

As the sun set, he brought up the dinner he'd ordered—salad, cold lobster, and cheesecake—and they ate in indolent leisure. Now, though, he was through waiting. His cock was so hard and thick it about pushed a hole in his shorts, and, unless Lee was blind—which she wasn't—she couldn't avoid seeing it. He thought of all the casual ways he could lead into this, but he was way past casual. He just needed to keep reminding himself this wasn't a session at Ultra. That she had no idea about that side of him.

They were standing at the rail, watching the last of the sun dip below the horizon, so it was easy to turn her into his arms and took her mouth. Her lips were lush and full, and she tasted of margaritas and lobster and cheesecake and woman. His tongue slicked against hers, dancing with it, sliding into the corners of her mouth and licking up every flavor. He waited a heartbeat to see if she'd push him away, but, no, it seemed she'd come here as intent on this as he was. He freed her ponytail and wound his fingers in her hair, sifting the silk of it before clutching her head in place. Her arms wound around him, her fingers stroking the nape of his neck, lighting his nerve endings.

And, just that fast, he was on fire.

With some effort, he broke the kiss. "Let's take this downstairs."

Fire danced in her eyes when she looked at him, and, when she spoke, her breathing was uneven.

"All right. Yes. Okay."

He was glad the bed in the master stateroom was king-sized. He liked a lot of room to play. He stood her at the side of the bed and untied the strings of the bathing suit top and tossed it to the side. Then, stripping back the covers, he deposited her on the sheet and laid her back against the pillows, hair spread out around her like a dark cloud. Her breasts were creamy mounds with tips a deep rosy color. He bent low and took one into his mouth, sucking on it hard before scraping it with his teeth. He was rewarded with a gasp of pleasure from Lee, so he gave the same treatment to the other nipple. By the time he finished with both of them, kneading her flesh while he sucked and nipped, she was panting, and he hadn't even moved below the waist.

Jesus!

He'd love to see her bent backward over a curved board, wrists manacled at her sides while he tormented her breasts until she came from nothing more than his touch. Maybe he'd clamp her nipples for additional pleasure—hers and his. God. He needed to turn his brain off because this wasn't the time to let his imagination run away from him. This was the time for seduction so he could move forward with his plan.

At last he forced himself to shift lower, untie and toss away the miniscule bottom of the suit, and then he stared at her gorgeous mound. Every inch of skin was carefully waxed except for two thin strips of dark brown curls defining each labium. He trailed the tip of one finger between those plump pussy lips, gathering the moisture there then lifting his finger to his mouth and sucking it slowly. Lee watched him, sliding her tongue across her lower lip. The ache in his dick increased tenfold. Spreading her labia, he bent down and ran his tongue along the same path his finger had taken. She was soaked, a sure sign she'd been aroused for some time.

"So beautiful," he murmured. "Such a nice shade of pink. God. I have to have a taste."

He lapped up every bit of her moisture, swirling his tongue around her clit, now a dark pink. He gave it the same treatment he'd given to her nipples, sucking hard on it and grazing it with his teeth, biting a little, then soothing with his tongue. He had to hold her hips in place because the more he sucked and nipped, the more she moved beneath him, thrusting her hips at him to bring her pussy in closer contact with his mouth.

"What do you want, Lee?" He looked at her skin flushed with arousal. "Tell me. Tell me what you need."

"You inside me," she panted. "Now."

He laughed low in his throat. "I'll bet you do, but we're a long way from there. By the time I'm inside you, you'll be begging me to do anything to you I want."

"Cocky, aren't you?" She gasped, even as she wriggled in his grasp and urged him with silent signals to stop talking and get busy again.

"As a matter of fact, yes." He took one of her hands and placed it right on his penis. "See how cocky I am?"

"Then we need to make use of it." Her voice shook with need.

"Oh, I promise you we will."

He put his mouth on her again, this time going straight for the little bundle of nerves that had turned even darker as blood surged to the tissues. Drawing her labia apart with his thumbs to give him better access, he was about to take a small bite of it when something caught his eyes. He stared, stared harder, and then moved one hand so he could examine her clit more closely. Was that evidence of a piercing? *Shit!* Of course it was. Not for Lee Sullivan but for Mistress Star. He stopped himself before he could say anything, unwilling to break the flow of what was happening by having her alternate personality intrude. They'd get around to it sooner rather than later.

She tugged on his hair, pulling his head down again, a silent urging to get back to what he was doing. He took his time, tracing every inch of her outer flesh with his tongue, lapping with slow strokes, nibbling, then lapping again until the muscles in her body tightened and she arched her hips to him. It had been so long since he'd had vanilla sex, he wasn't sure he could do it right, but he was damn sure giving it his best shot.

"Touch your clit for me," he told her in a voice rough with lust. "Please."

When she still hadn't moved her hand, he realized giving orders to a Mistress wasn't the way to go. He needed to dial back his Dom voice, or this might be over when it had barely even started.

"Please, Lee. I want to watch. Show me how you rub yourself."

She moved one hand from his head to her stomach, slid it with deliberation down her skin to where he held her pussy open, and brushed the tip of a finger over her hot button.

"That's it." He was doing his best to keep a lid on his Dom voice. It was nowhere near time for that, yet he wanted her to do what he said. "Do it, Lee. Rub faster. Harder."

When he lifted his gaze, he saw her looking down at him from beneath the long sweep of her lashes, her eyes heavy with desire. She moved her hand again, picking up the rhythm and rubbing the dark pink flesh, giving it a light pinch then rubbing again. When her breathing accelerated and her hips moved in a hitching motion, he slid his hands beneath the rounded cheeks of her ass. Lifting her, he placed his mouth right over her opening. When he thrust his tongue inside, she cried out and pushed herself up to him.

She was so hot and wet inside, so tasty and juicy, he could have done this forever. In fact, if she had been playing as his sub, he would have dragged it out until she begged and pleaded with him to let her come. But, again, that wasn't for tonight. Her inner walls flexed and pulsed around his tongue, and her fingers moved faster on her clit. Tightening his grip on her hips to hold her in place, he increased the pace of his tongue to match her hand.

"Ohhh!"

The cry burst from her lips as her pussy clamped down on his tongue, and she bucked in his grip.

Her body shook, the walls of her cunt spasmed, and her cream flooded his tongue. He sucked it in as fast as he could while he continued to ride her through her orgasm. At last she was limp in his grasp, the sound of her breathing raw in the still air. Still he licked inside her channel, scooping every last drop from her, running his tongue back and forth over her sweet spot.

'I'm dead." Her voice was giddy, her breath stuttering.

"Is that all you've got?" he teased and ran his fingertips over her slit with a whisper of a touch.

She jerked in response. "A moment, please. Okay?"

"I'll even give you a few."

He hitched himself up so he had access to her breasts and took one of her delicious nipples in his mouth. Again the image of them clamped, maybe with weights tugging them down, sent a bolt of lust spearing through his body. His cock twitched in response, but he kept to his task, sucking and biting as he'd done before, kneading her breasts as he did so. When she laced her fingers through his hair again, tugging on the strands, he lifted his gaze and caught the red flush of desire on her face and the heavy flutter of her pulse at the hollow of her throat.

Impulsively, he moved enough so he could close his mouth over it and suck, hard. He swallowed a smile of satisfaction, knowing Lee was not used to a situation she did not control. That made this all that much sweeter. And made him twice as hot.

When her breathing evened out and her pulse rate slackened, he turned his attention back to her pussy, now flushed to a rosy pink. He couldn't resist taking a little nip at her clit, swollen and darker than the flesh surrounding it. When he clamped his teeth down on it, Lee jackknifed up and grabbed his head.

"No."

Oh, yeah, there was her Mistress Star voice. God, how it turned him on. He ignored her and kept at his task, tormenting the ultrasensitive nub of nerves.

"I said no," she repeated.

Braceleting her wrists with his fingers, he held tight to her while he worked away, calling all those nerves to life again, lapping at a fresh spate of cream.

"Give me one more," he mumbled, his mouth against her heated flesh.

She tried to wriggle away from his grasp, but he held tight, thrusting his tongue inside her again. Fucking her with it until he felt the next climax exploding from her.

She collapsed back on the pillows, panting. "I suppose you think you're in charge here."

He lifted her hands, his fingers still wrapped around her wrists, and grinned at her. "I'd say I know who's in charge."

She tried to yank her hands away. "So that's how it's going to be?"

He laughed. "Count on it." He pulled himself up until his face was a scant inch from hers. "And think how much fun it will be."

He was delighted she couldn't quite put Mistress Star away, even in a vanilla situation. God, he could only imagine how she'd be when—

She grabbed his head, pulled it down, and thrust her tongue inside his mouth, lapping all the inner surfaces, rubbing her tongue over his. He felt her hot, sweet breath on his face, the pressure of her breasts against his chest. Then, as he was about to take the kiss even deeper, she yanked her hands free, pushed hard, and rolled them over so he was on his back. Before he even realized what had happened, she was straddling him, and now it was his wrists imprisoned. He could hardly wait to see what she would do now, what her next move would be.

The smile she gave him was nothing short of lascivious. Giving her lower lip an indolent swipe with her tongue, she released his wrists and tugged up the bottom of his T-shirt until his chest was exposed. She stared at it for a long moment before raking her nails through the dusting of hair down to the waist of his shorts. The skim of her nails sent shivers racing over his skin, and his hard cock flexed against her bottom. Her lips curved in a knowing smile.

She bent down and closed her teeth around one of his nipples, the same way he'd done to her. Streaks of heat sizzled through him, so intense he wondered how much longer he'd be able to play out this little game. He forced himself to hold still while she teased him with her teeth and lips, moving from one hard nipple to the other, stroking him with her hands while she worked her mouth on him. At the moment he was about to yank her away, she sat upright.

"You have too many clothes on. Take them off."

"You want them off?" he challenged her. "You do it."

For a moment he thought she'd refuse, but she grabbed his shirt and maneuvered it over his head, tossing it to the side. The shorts were a little more complicated, made more so since he lay there with his hands clasped behind his head, daring her to ask for his help. She scooted down his legs, popping open the button and lowering the zipper. When she parted the fabric and his cock sprang free, he was pleased to note a slight widening of her eyes. He knew he was well endowed, more so than many other men he'd seen in locker rooms and at Ultra. He couldn't wait to see how tight he fit inside her.

With no more than a few gymnastics, she managed to remove his shorts and boxer briefs and position herself back on her knees. When she wrapped her slim fingers around his shaft, he sucked in a breath. Then she bent and took him into her mouth, closing her lips around him and sucking, and his eyes crossed. Holy shit! She might look like an angel, but she had the mouth of a devil, hot and wicked, almost scorching the tender skin of his cock. When she slipped the other hand between his thighs and cupped his balls, his breath lodged in his throat.

"I think that's enough." He tangled his fingers in her hair and tried to pull her head away.

She laughed, the vibrations reverberating through his penis and his balls, and shook her head, lips still wrapped around him.

Okay, he was past waiting out this battle of wills. He wanted to fuck her more than he wanted his next breath. He managed to pull her head away from him without doing himself bodily harm and flipped her onto her back. He knew she was more than ready because her pussy had left moisture on his thighs. In seconds, he'd fished a condom from the nightstand next to the bed, ripped open the foil, and rolled on the latex. Driven by a sudden fierce need, he lifted her legs and pushed them back so she was wide open to him, positioned himself at her opening, and drove into her with one hard thrust.

Jesus, she was tight. Holy shit! As her hot, wet walls clamped around him like a vise, he had to stop and draw a breath to collect himself. He didn't want this to be over before it started. He locked his gaze with hers, seeing the same fierceness, the same ravenous look reflected there he felt himself. With his hands behind her knees, he pushed her legs back to open her even more, drew back a tiny bit and rammed home again.

He closed his eyes for one moment, enjoying the feel of her around him, but then urgency took over, shredding his famous self-control. He pounded into her, all finesse gone as he drove her up that high, slick wall to fulfillment. She was right there with him on the fast ride, gripping his biceps to balance herself, hips moving in the fast rhythm he'd established. When she freed her legs, wound them around his waist, and locked her ankles at the small of his back, pulling him in even deeper, he had to grit his teeth to keep from exploding. He watched her eyes for the signal, the sign, and when he saw it, he drove into her once more, hard and deep, and took them over the edge of that wall in a wild freefall.

The heavy pounding of his heart and the rough seesaw of his breath couldn't disguise the fact that, despite his best intentions, this was turning into something more than just sex.

And he needed to fix that right away.

Chapter Six

Lee leaned back in the tub, letting the masses of soap bubbles bounce against her skin and inhaling the faint scent of lavender from the bath salts she used. Over the past three weeks, her body had seen more activity than it had in months, and she wasn't sure if she was pleased or not. There was nothing gentle about Branch Colby as a lover. He was inventive, demanding, even controlling, which led to a continual battle of wills. Most of the time, she enjoyed the push and pull. It was a nice change from the men who submitted to her, even those like Drew, who made it interesting by always holding a little something of himself back. She could never see Branch as a sub. He had too much of the Dom in him. This, however—whatever it was—made for an interesting change-up.

Interesting. Yes, that was the word. Each time they'd been together, he'd eased a little taste of BDSM into their sexual activities. Suggested a little of this and a little of that. He'd heard about something. Read about something. Not that she expected a man like Branch Colby to be sexually unsophisticated.

Besides, these days a lot of vanilla people often thought to spice up their lives by dipping their toe in the waters. Always in the privacy of their own bedrooms, of course. From the little Branch had slipped into their evenings together, she figured he was fascinated enough by it, like a lot of men, to experiment with it if he believed his partner was willing. She couldn't deny the sex between them was scorching.

But that wasn't all it was, and that was nice, too. He had taken her to dinner at some very intimate, high-end places and out for another ride on his "small boat." The past two Saturdays they'd gone exploring in the small towns around San Antonio. Who would have thought Branch Colby collected Western antiques? Last Sunday he'd shown up with pizza, and they'd watched football together.

And, of course, there had been the sex—plentiful and spectacular. He was an inventive lover who enjoyed all aspects of sex. What made it more enticing was the constant battle between them for control. More and more, she saw the Dom in him, and she wondered if, when he wasn't with her, he gave full rein to it. Somehow, strange as it seemed, she had a sense they were both winning the battle.

The thing that shocked her the most was that, against all expectations, she found her emotions coming into play, with a man who didn't do emotional attachments or lasting relationships. And neither did she. She'd long ago given up looking for or expecting one. Men who weren't submissives didn't connect with her. And most of them resented a woman taking charge in bed. How was she supposed to handle what was happening now? What should she do with her own emotions? Sooner rather than later, she knew she'd have to end this. Wouldn't she? Could they somehow make this work, two such controlling personalities? In any event, she planned to enjoy it as long as she could. Tonight they would be staying in. Casual, he told her. At home. A nice, relaxed evening. Come and spend the night.

And have lots of sex.

Enjoy it, Lee. Don't give yourself a headache. Enjoy the fact a man like Branch Colby is attracted to you and wants to spend time with you. Worry about the fallout later.

She had managed to take the edge off her needs with a few scattered visits to Infinity, but even that had left her with an unfinished feeling. Branch Colby was different from most of the men she dated outside the club. The money might have been part of it but not all of it, although god knew he had enough for a small country. Maybe it was the absence of his need to impress her. He drove an SUV instead of a high-dollar vehicle. He seemed to enjoy dinner at a highway diner more than the most expensive restaurant in the city. And he didn't have an air of entitlement. That was it. He was just plain unimpressed with himself.

Again, she gave herself a jolt of reality. She couldn't afford to develop real feelings or a sense of attachment to Branch. However he acted with her, men like him didn't marry women like her or, in his case, maybe any woman at all. No, the vibes he gave off, despite the other pleasant times they'd spent together, were of a man who based his personal life on sex and nothing more. He certainly gave no indication he was a man looking to settle down. She'd had the sense from the beginning that this was an adventure based on sex, and, damn, the sex was good. More than good. Spectacular, even.

But marry? Was she crazy? Where had that thought come from anyway? She needed to quit letting her brain run away from her, get out of the tub, and get dressed for the evening. Branch had tried to insist on picking her up, but she wanted her own transportation. He'd told her he hoped she'd stay the night with him, something she'd avoided so far. Going home to her own bed gave her the feeling of being in control of the situation. She didn't know if she was ready to take this to another level or put an end to it, and she wasn't used to having her emotions all over the place like this or being so indecisive. All she could do was see how it played out. Having her car there was her safety valve. It gave her a sense of security. She could leave any time she wanted to.

So get with the program, she told herself. *And stop looking for trouble where there isn't any.*

***

He checked everything one last time. The wine was chilling. The finger foods were ready in the fridge. He had a stack of CDs ready to go at the push of a button and, in his bedroom, an interesting assortment of toys that he hoped he'd get to use. Now he paced back and forth from the kitchen to the foyer and back again. He was edgy and impatient. Edgy because, out of nowhere, he had misgivings about what he'd planned for tonight and impatient because he was eager to see Lee.

And that fact made him even edgier. At his age,

he'd had more than his share of women. Maybe someone else's, too. He thought back to his conversation with Max when the discussion of Lee had first come up and the things Max had said. It was true the women he dated outside Ultra occupied him for a short while, but he'd come to realize they were interchangeable. His attraction to them faded fast, however, and it had become harder and harder to find one who held his interest. Lee had become the exception to the rule, and it made him uneasy about his plans for the evening.

Because something had entered into the equation he hadn't expected—emotions. And he had no idea what to do with them. He'd spent so many years guarding his heart from the women who wanted to use him as much as he used them, the ones who lusted after his money and position, now he was afraid to let it break free.

Go figure, he told himself. Just when he least expected it—when he least needed it—that four-letter word, *love*, had imprinted itself on him like a brand. He had never trusted it, kept himself immune to it, but that made this all the more shocking. He was not prepared for this at all. What had started out as a sexual adventure had turned into something so deep, so emotional, he had no idea what to do with it.

Lee Sullivan was the ultimate self-possessed female. That was what had attracted him to begin with, a woman who could meet him on equal footing. He was positive she'd think he was nuts if he told her how he felt.

He had to get himself to square one, the reason for this little dance they'd been doing. He had seen her as a challenge, and now it was time to meet that challenge. If tonight worked out the way he expected, he'd win his bet, he and Lee would part friends with her none the wiser, and they would each go back to their separate, individual lives.

Tell that to someone who believes you, said the little devil in his head.

For that one moment, he was tempted to call the whole thing off. Never mind that Max would laugh his ass off. That wasn't what was important here. Was it?

He was standing in the foyer looking out the window next to the door when his cell rang. He pulled it from his pocket, looked at the screen, and saw Max's face.

"What?" he asked, his tone sharp. "I'm busy."

"Hey. Checking in to make sure tonight's the night. That's all."

Fuck. He wished to hell he'd never told Max this was it. Again, he even wished he'd never made the damn bet.

"It won't be anything if you don't leave me alone," he growled. "Good night, Max."

He disconnected the call and turned off the phone, uncertainty holding him in its unfamiliar grasp.

Don't be nuts. You may think she's different, but, in the end, she won't be any different from any of the other women.

That's what he had to hang onto. He had just shoved his cell in his pocket when he saw Lee's car head up the driveway and stop in front of the house. Smiling, he opened the door.

"I like a man who's anxious to see me." She grinned at him.

"Always. Come on in. I've got your favorite white on ice."

His cock sprang to life. It seemed all he had to do was look at her and he got hard as a rock. Her thick curtain of dark hair fell to her shoulders, and he couldn't resist brushing it back from her face and placing a light kiss on her cheek. The sheer blouse and tank top she wore did little to disguise the roundness of her breasts or the fact her nipples were already hard and poking against the material. He didn't remember ever being with a woman as hungry for sex as he was, not until Lee. He couldn't wait until later when he could get her clothes off and get her on her knees. And he definitely planned for that to happen.

By the time they'd had some wine and nibbled their way through their food, his cock and balls ached with anticipation with such anticipation he wasn't sure how much longer he cold last.. When she held out her wine goblet for a refill, he took the glass from her and set it on the table. The he stood up and urged her to her feet also.

"I can't wait any longer to get my hands on you tonight."

He cupped her cheeks, drawing her face to him, and licked her soft lips, one casual swipe of his tongue then another. With the tip he traced the closed seam of her mouth, back and forth until she opened for him, allowing him to sweep inside. Jesus, she always tasted so damn good. Not even the crisp flavor of the wine could disguise the taste that was distinctively Lee, and he drank his fill of her. She lifted her hands and threaded her fingers through his hair, taking the kiss deep and teasing his tongue to duel with hers.

At last, when he self-control was about to snap, he lifted his head. "Let's take this into the bedroom."

Something he couldn't define flashed in her eyes, and, for a moment, he thought she was going to refuse. Then she smiled at him, that smile that lit a fire in his blood, and she nodded her head. In his bedroom, he dove in for another kiss, sucking her tongue into his mouth and biting down on it with a gentle graze of his teeth. She gave as good as she got, her tongue as wicked as his. When he slipped his hands down her back to squeeze her buttocks she moaned, the sound soft as it drifted into his mouth.

Catching his breath, he took a step back. God, she was hot. Knowing she was a Domme—and that she was unaware he knew it—made this even more arousing.

"Are you up for a little game tonight?" he asked, his mouth as close to hers as it could get without touching.

"What kind of game?" She searched his eyes as if seeking some kind of hidden answer.

He dropped his gaze and instead focused on the heavy beat of the pulse in the hollow of her throat. *Damn!* She was already aroused, too.

He nipped along the edge of her jaw.

"What if I gave you orders tonight? Told you what to do instead of asking you?"

His tongue circled the inner shell of her ear, a touch he knew raised her temperature.

"Maybe even blindfolded you so every touch, every response, would be that much more intense?"

When she didn't say anything, he studied her face. "Afraid of me, Lee? Afraid of what I might make you do?"

He could almost see the battle she was raging with herself. A muscle twitched in the softness of her cheek, and she looked away from him, down at her feet. Not a submissive act but to hide her thoughts from him.

"Haven't you ever wondered," he asked, "what it would be like to put yourself completely at the mercy of a man for one night? A man that you trusted without reservation?"

She lifted her gaze, tiny flecks of gold shimmering in the deep hazel of her eyes.

"And that would be you?"

"If you trust me. Do you, Lee? Trust me?"

For a long, tension-filled moment, he was positive she would refuse him. That the turnabout would be too much for her. As far as she knew, he had no knowledge of her life as Mistress Star, so he couldn't just suggest a switch of roles. Besides, for reasons far beyond his bet with Max, he wanted her to want this.

A slow, hungry smile tilted her lips, and the anxiety eased from his body.

"I do. And I think that might be—interesting."

He blew out a breath and took a step back. "Very well, then. Remove your clothing, all of it, but don't rush it. One piece at a time."

He was surprised to see that her hands shook a bit as she lifted them, but then they steadied. With deliberate movements, she untied the tails of the sheer overblouse, let them fall, and unbuttoned the two closed buttons. Her focus never left Branch's as she shrugged the garment from her shoulders and tossed it onto a chair next to the bed. The soft material of her tank top outlined the hard buds of her nipples. She waited for a moment, letting Branch look his fill, before she tugged the cami over her head.

Lee stood there, waiting until his eyes had raked over her before unclasping her bra and setting her breasts free.

Branch sucked in a breath, his mouth watering at the sight of her taut buds. He stepped forward and placed a hot kiss where her neck and shoulder joined, followed by a tiny bite. Then he did the same to the other side.

When he moved away, she slid her feet out of her sandals and eased herself out of her slacks and her thong. He watched every movement she made, admiring her gracefulness. He recognized the total control and lack of self-consciousness of a natural Domme. He had to resist the urge to lick his lips.

When at last she was naked, he took the opportunity to study her body, not that he hadn't seen it so many times already. He loved the proud uptilt of her breasts, the dark rosiness of her nipples and the aureoles surrounding them. The slight curve of her stomach and the sweep of her hips to her thighs. The light he'd left on made the neat rows of curls on her mound glint, already dampened with her moisture. Lee Sullivan was a passionate woman easily aroused when she had her shields down. He wondered if any other man had ever discovered that side of Lee, then hated himself for the brief slash of jealousy.

She stood there, hands at her sides, relaxed, the corners of her mouth upturned with the hint of a smile. Challenging him, the minx. He swallowed his own smile.

"Spread your legs apart then touch your pussy and show me how wet your finger is."

She moved her feet farther apart, drew her finger through her slit, and held it up for his observation as he'd ordered. Her cream glistened in the light.

"Excellent. Now lick it clean for me." He needed to see how far he could push her with nothing more than commands before he moved to anything else. His own problem was keeping his cock and his raging hunger for her under control.

Still watching him, she ran her tongue in a lazy swipe over her finger, turning it to catch every surface then holding it out for his inspection. He moved close enough to grasp her hand and close his mouth over the same finger. The smile was gone from her lips but not the insolence. That turned him on even more.

"Turn around, bend over, and grab your ankles. I don't think I've taken a good enough look at how well you trim the hair around your cunt."

Again she hesitated for a moment, a hint of insouciance in her eyes, but then she turned and bent over. Branch sucked in his breath at the sight of her, pink pussy lips shiny with her juice, the thin strip of hair outlining her opening. Her tiny rear opening winked at him between the cheeks of her buttocks, and it was all he could do to restrain himself from falling to his knees and plunging his cock into her and at the same time teasing her rear opening with his tongue. He had to clear his throat twice before he could speak.

"I think you haven't displayed the proper attitude." He ran a hand over the curve of her ass.

"Do you know what I do with...women... who are disobedient or too arrogant?"

"What would that be?" God, she still had a hint of laughter in her voice. He loved the way she challenged him.

"I spank them. Like this." He smacked one cheek of her buttocks hard enough to leave a handprint. "And like this." He slapped the other one.

She rocked forward but never lost her balance. "Do you find it necessary to do that often?"

"You are an insolent one. Do you find that works for you?"

She laughed, the little tease. "More than you might imagine."

He slapped both cheeks again and then again. When she tipped forward this time, he reached between her arms and her body and closed a hand over one breast. He squeezed it, hard, and was rewarded with a sharp intake of her breath. Sliding the hand upward, he closed it around her neck and urged her to stand upright. He cupped her chin and turned her so she faced him.

"Shall we add a little spice to the mix, stubborn minx?"

"I thought that's what we were doing." She considered his face, the look in her eyes as bold as ever. "Are we playing a different kind of game here, Branch? If so, maybe you should tell me the rules."

He ran his fingers through her hair, holding her head in place, preventing her from looking away from him.

"How about this? If I said I wanted you blindfolded, on your knees, hands cuffed behind your back while you suck my cock, what would you say to that?"

"What would you want me to say?"

Jesus! If ever there was a woman who could get him to submit it would be her, but that wasn't on the program tonight.

"I'd want you to say yes. And thank me."

"Do you do this a lot?" she asked.

"That's not what we're discussing. We're discussing the here and now. *Right* now. So tell me. What's your answer?"

He could almost see the wheels turning in her head while she decided how to respond. Would she decide that, for one night, it would be fun to have a role reversal? And right at that moment, he wondered which of them was in control.

She licked her lips, stared hard at him for a moment, then nodded her head. "My answer is yes."

For a second he thought his heart would leap from his chest with excitement. Thank god he had great self-control.

"Excellent. Stay right where you are. Do not move even one inch. And place your hands behind your back."

He had no idea why she was being so agreeable about this, but she did what he ordered her to do without exception or variation, even to the placement of her hands. He pulled a silk square and a set of handcuffs from the dresser drawer where he kept some of his toys. He hesitated a moment before lifting a small flogger and adding it to the items. When he looked back at Lee, she hadn't moved, but her eyes took in everything he was doing.

"Are you thinking of using that little thing also?" she asked.

"And if I said yes?"

"I'd ask you why and also how you happened to have it so handy."

He walked over to stand in front of her. "Maybe this is really how I like my sex. What would you say to that?"

Another hint of a grin. "Maybe I'd say bring it on."

Jesus! He had never met a woman like this. He might get her to submit, but she'd never be a submissive. She would challenge him all the time, both in the bedroom and out, and make him enjoy every minute of it. No wonder she was so good at her job.

Okay, no more word games, except for one.

"Give me a word, any word, that you'll use any time you want to stop. Whatever it is, whenever you use it, I will respect it."

She gave her lips a lazy swipe with her tongue, and what he thought might be \mischief sparked in her eyes?

"Sandstorm."

He quirked an eyebrow. "Really?"

She shrugged one shoulder, a slight, graceful move. "It just popped into my head."

"Okay, sandstorm it is."

He put the items on his bed then undressed, watching her reaction as each piece of clothing came off. Other than a widening of her eyes and a twitch of her hands when he took off his boxer briefs and his cock sprang free, she didn't move so much as a tony muscle.

"You know," he said in a conversational tone, "when you remove one sense, the rest of them become much more sensitive and intense." He folded the square into a blindfold, placed it over her eyes, and tied it behind her head. "What do you smell now?"

She inhaled. "Spicy aftershave, male musk. She drew in another breath. "Mint, I'd say from soap."

"Excellent. Open your mouth." He touched the head of his cock, scooped the tiny bead of fluid sitting on the slit, and held his finger to her mouth. "What do you taste?" He placed his fingertip on her tongue.

She closed her lips over his finger. "Your cum. Salty and a little sweet."

He walked around behind her and slipped the manacles around her wrists. Locked them. "What do you hear? Feel?"

"The sound of metal on metal, touching my hands."

"On your knees," he snapped. "Now."

He couldn't believe how graceful she was, barely losing her balance. He wondered what kind of calisthenics she performed with her subs.

"Mouth open," he ordered.

She opened her mouth wide, and when he placed the head of his cock on her lower lip, she moved forward a tiny amount but enough to take him into her mouth. Gripping her head to steady it and hold it in place, he rode her lips, sucking in a breath when she closed them around his shaft and sucked until her cheeks hollowed. He didn't want to think who else had been treated to this extraordinary skill of hers. All he wanted was to enjoy it at the moment, and enjoyment was too simple a word for what he felt. Her talented mouth sent waves of pleasure through him until his entire focus was on his cock and what was happening.

When he felt the familiar tightening of the muscles at the small of his back and in his balls, he tried to hold off his climax, wanting to prolong this as long as possible. But there was no holding back from what she was doing to him. He tightened his fingers on her jaw and stiffened his body as the orgasm roared through him. Spurt after spurt of his cum landed on her tongue, her throat muscles flexing as she swallowed every drop. When she'd drained him dry, he loosened his hold and stepped back, easing his penis from her mouth. When she ran her tongue over her lips and made a humming sound, unbelievably his cock tried to spring to life again.

Branch took a moment to settle himself, to reach into the Dom part of him, so he could maintain control in this situation. Or at least think he could. Then he helped Lee rise to her feet.

"Very well done." He caught himself before the word "sub" slipped from his mouth. "And here is your reward."

He bent her over the edge of the bed and arranged her face down, head turned. The imprint of his hand on her ass hadn't yet faded, and the temptation was too great to resist. She jolted when the first slap landed then curled her hands into fists, digging her fingers into her palms. With her hands manacled behind her back, she was helpless and open to him, a situation that sent a surge of lust through him.

He landed another spanking and another until, this time, her buttocks became a bright shade of red and her nails had dug crescents into her palms. She was so turned on, he could smell her scent. If the two of them stayed together, their lives would never be dull, and the sex would top the charts.

Wait a minute. Stay together? Not on the agenda.

He slid his fingers down the crevice between her buttocks, pausing to press the tip of a finger at the opening of her rear channel. God, how he'd love to fuck her there, although he was pretty sure it wasn't happening tonight.

Spreading her legs, he knelt between them, pushed her thighs wide apart, and put his mouth to her cunt. A slight jerk of her body was her only response to the touch of his mouth until he began to work her in earnest. He licked all around her opening, flattened his tongue to press it beneath her labia and find her clit, rubbing the tip over it again and again. God, she was a wet one, so responsive as her cream flooded her channel. He teased her clit again and again until her control began to fray and her hips thrust back at him. He gripped her thighs to hold her still and plunged his tongue inside her.

She got juicier and juicier, her taste an aphrodisiac on his tongue. He lapped and sucked, wondering who was enjoying this the most. Again and again he drove her to the edge until he had her squirming on the bed, panting, and at last even begging. Then he slid the handle of the flogger into her very ready pussy and pinched her clit hard, sending her over the edge. Her involuntary scream of pleasure was the sweetest music he'd ever heard.

He rose and rested his hands on her sweet, upturned ass. She was incredible, beyond his wildest expectations. And the night was far from over. Only...for a fleeting moment, he wondered who was in fact in charge here.

Chapter Seven

Lee set her mug of coffee down on the vanity and stared at herself in the bathroom mirror. Nope, no change. She looked the same as she had when she left home Saturday night to go to Branch's. She might feel like a different person but it didn't mean she looked like one. Not that there had been many changes, but holy crap! Branch Colby had taken her on a sexual journey she'd never expected to travel.

There was no doubt the man was a Dom, no matter what he did or didn't say. Not at Infinity or she would have seen him before. There were two other high-end clubs in the area, though, so he could be a member at either of them. Maybe she would ask John Francona a casual question or two about him. John was a walking encyclopedia of who and what in the BDSM lifestyle for the entire area.

She'd bet his subs lined up for sessions with him, although that wasn't a role she could ever play. It just wasn't part of her genetic makeup. She had learned that without question when going through her training. Could she pretend for one evening, though? *God!* What an erotic trip. Even now, on Monday morning, even after a long bath yesterday, she still had pleasant aches in secret places. Aches that brought a smile to her face. Would she do it again? Not on a regular basis, but for an exciting change? Sure. Only not with just anyone. It had to be someone with whom she shared a special connection.

So where did that leave her with Branch Colby? Did they share that connection? Was it too soon to tell, or had it happened without her realizing it?

Even as she thought about him, her cell rang, and she saw his name displayed on the screen.

"Morning." His deep voice resonated even through the telephone.

"Same to you." She took a sip of coffee.

"Feeling okay today?" The heat of his voice seeped through the telephone and into her body.

"Fine." Oh, yes, most fine. "And you?"

He laughed, a warm, relaxed sound. "Never better. And that very nice ass of yours?"

Lee couldn't believe she felt herself blush. "My ass is doing great, too."

"Glad to hear it." He paused. "Listen, I wondered if you were free for lunch today."

"Lunch?" So he wanted to move forward with this—whatever it was? "Maybe. It turns out I have a meeting in your building around eleven-thirty. The chairman of the mayor's fundraising committee has offices there."

"How about coming up here when you're finished? I can have lunch ordered in, or we can go out somewhere. Your choice."

She nibbled her lip. She didn't have much time, but lunch with him was so tempting.

"I'll be kind of pressed for time," she told him.

"I'm guessing my meeting will last an hour, and I have to be back at my office by two. Ordering in sounds good."

"How about texting me when your meeting is about to wrap up so I can order the food? Any preferences?"

She shook her head before remembering he couldn't see her. "Anything light would be fine."

"I'll do it. See you then."

She put the cell back down on the vanity and stared at herself again in the mirror. Somehow she expected to see a change in her face, some sign of the incredible sex or the indefinable connection she felt with Branch. That one Saturday night had made both more intense and more complicated. No, she still looked like the same Lee Sullivan. Oh, maybe there was a new heat simmering in her eyes or a new awareness of herself. And maybe her dreams last night had been filled with a very sexy man and the outrageous things he'd done with and to her.

And the emotions he stirred in her.

But her outward appearance seemed the same. Good. What had she expected, a sign emblazoned across her forehead that said *Lee likes punishment*?

And another thing. Saturday night had reawakened in her something she'd discovered during her training—she enjoyed pain. It stimulated her pheromones and ramped up the responses of her body. The big difference, for her, was she never fell into subspace. She could embrace the pain but still, at all times, be in control of her mind.

What if Branch wanted to do this more? If he wanted something exclusive? Was she ready for that with him? She'd thought she had her life organized, her future planned, and it didn't include a permanent relationship with a man who was a Dom, whether overtly or not.

Damn, Lee. Indecisive much?

First, she needed to sort out what her real feelings for him were.

After taking a final sip of coffee, she pulled her hair back into a ponytail and turned on the shower. Maybe the hot water would wash away the jumble of thoughts in her brain so she could function today.

***

Branch signed off the Skype conference he'd participated in and turned his chair to stare out the glass wall at his favorite view. No, wrong. His favorite view was Lee Sullivan, naked in his bedroom, her ass bright red, writhing in the throes of orgasm. Or sitting cross-legged next to him on the couch, crunching potato chips and screaming at the football game on television. It seemed she fit whatever area of his life he introduced her to like a well-designed glove.

Yesterday morning when he'd woken up with her in his bed, curled into him, the scent of her hair tickling his nose, her perfume imprinted on his pillows, he'd had a sense of peace he couldn't ever remember feeling. And this morning, when he'd woken up alone? Her absence was even more acute. How had this whole thing sneaked up on him this way? How had he reached the point where he wanted her in his life all the time so quickly?

Did she feel the same way? Did she want to explore this further and see what they had?

"Knock knock."

Branch looked up to see Max standing in his doorway.

"Come on in."

He saved the spreadsheet on his computer and turned in his chair.

"Karen wasn't at her desk, so I barged in. You real busy now?"

Branch shook his head. "Yes, but no. I need a break from looking at these numbers."

He had been expecting this. Max knew Lee had spent Saturday night at his house and was no doubt after an update on that stupid bet. And it was stupid. Idiotic. What had he even been thinking? He hadn't been; that was the problem. His ego had gotten in the way. Even then, it might not have been a problem if the situation with Lee Sullivan hadn't taken a wild and unexpected turn. He had long ago given up finding a woman who could live comfortably in his world without being impressed by it. Or by him. A woman who was smart, sexy, funny, and could adapt to any situation. There was no artifice about Lee Sullivan. She was the genuine article, no doubt about that, and far more than his dick was involved here.

Which was why he was uncomfortable knowing Max wanted answers to questions.

He looked at his watch. "All I've got is a few minutes. Lee has a meeting in this building, and I expect her to text me any minute that she's finished so I can order lunch."

"This won't take long." His friend dropped into a chair opposite the desk. "I just want to know if I won my bet, or if I have to fork over the cash."

"I could say that a gentleman never tells," Branch joked. "Maybe you were right. Maybe it was a stupid bet to make."

Max looked at him with a quizzical expression. "Are you saying it did happen, or it didn't? You're being very mysterious, my friend."

Branch shrugged. "Maybe there's nothing to tell yet."

Max threw back his head and laughed. "Nice try. You've been with this woman for almost a month. I know damn well you've had sex and knowing you, plenty of it. So did you get her to do it? Submit to you for one night? Don't forget. Four hundred grand rides on your answer since you were stupid enough to double down on it. Twice."

"I repeat. There's nothing to tell." He'd already decided to pay off the bet and keep the details to himself. Lee's privacy had become much more important to him.

"Come on, Branch. Did you get Mistress Star on her knees, submitting to you for one night? I'll tell you, there are a lot of men who'll be over the top envious of you. Too bad I can't share the details."

"Damn it, Max. Enough. There are no details. And by the way, can you keep it down a little here? We're in my office."

Branch came out from behind the desk to make sure the door between his office and Karen's was shut tight. When he saw that it hadn't quite closed, he decided to check and make sure Lee wasn't somehow on the other side. She had said she'd text him but—

When he yanked the door all the way open, he came face to face with Karen, who was getting ready to knock. She had a strange look on her face, and his first thought was to wonder if she had heard any of their conversation.

"Oh, Branch." She frowned. "Did something just happen in here?"

"Happen?" He lifted an eyebrow. "I have no idea what you mean."

"Miss Sullivan ran out of here like a fire was chasing her. I told her you were waiting for her, but all she said was to tell you she's changed her mind. You can stop waiting. Oh, and she asked me to delete her number from your cell phone. For god's sake, Branch, what did you do?"

"Something more stupid than you can imagine."

A knot lodged itself in Branch's stomach. Damn Max for not shutting the door all the way when he came in. And damn himself for not checking. Or telling Max to shut up. Why hadn't Lee texted as she'd told him she would? He grabbed his cell phone and realized he'd turned it off during a Skype meeting and, ass that he was, hadn't turned it back on.

Fuck, fuck, fuck.

"What's wrong?" Max asked, rising from his chair.

"Everything," Branch snapped. "Every fucking thing is wrong. I'm an idiot. Damn it all to hell." He glared at the other man. "I owe you four hundred grand. Nothing happened. You were right. And it was a stupid fucking bet. If I could, I'd kick myself in the ass."

Max's jaw dropped. "So you lost? I'm stunned."

Branch wanted to smack him. No, he wanted to smack himself.

"Just shut the fuck up."

"Wow. Lot of F-bombs today, Branch."

Branch stuffed his cell in his pocket and barreled out of the office, stopping just short of knocking

Karen over.

"Will you be back?" she called after him.

"I have no idea. Tell everyone I lost my mind and went to find it."

Impatient and agitated, he jiggled his keys as he waited for the elevator. How in hell could he have been such a blind idiot? Max had been right when he said one of these days he'd meet a woman who pushed all his buttons and his habit would backfire. Blow up in his face would be a more apt description.

He fidgeted as he rode the elevator down to the underground parking and raced to his SUV. His hand shook so much when he tried to put the key in the ignition that he dropped the key ring twice. As he pulled out into traffic, he tried to figure where she'd go. Back to work? Home? Someplace else?

He activated the hands-free option on his cell and tried Mayor Vincent's office first.

"I'm sorry, Mr. Colby," the receptionist told him. "Miss Sullivan called a few minutes ago and said she wouldn't be back today. She asked me to cancel her appointments. Can I take a message for her?"

Fuck! Fuck, fuck, fuck!

He tried her cell next, but it went straight to voice mail. Same with her townhouse number. He pounded his fist on the steering wheel. Okay, he'd just chase her down. Make her talk to him. Explain what an asshole jerk he'd been. Whatever it took.

As he raced through the city, he berated himself for the idiot he was. Max had warned him a woman would come along who would pierce all the shields around his heart and he'd manage to somehow fuck it up. God, how true that was. For a smart man, he was a stupid, stupid idiot.

He pulled up in front of her townhouse, screeching to a halt and getting out of the SUV while it was still rocking from the force of the abrupt stop. Her car was nowhere in sight but he knew these particular townhouses had covered resident parking in the rear so that didn't put him off. Long strides took him to the tiny porch, where he jammed his finger on the doorbell. When no one came to the door, he pressed it again and again, waiting just seconds to hear if anyone was moving around inside. Nothing. Next he pounded on the door as hard as he could.

"Lee. Lee, if you're in there, please open the door. I need to talk to you. Explain. Lee. Come on."

Pound, pound, pound.

Nothing.

"Lee." He stepped back on the deck and looked at the upper windows. "Lee, damn it. Open the door and let me talk to you."

Still nothing.

He reached over the fence to unlatch the gate leading to her small backyard. A sliding door led out to a patio, and he pressed his face to the glass, attempting to see inside. All he saw was an empty kitchen and part of the living room. Okay, maybe she was in her bedroom, but that was upstairs. Damn! He tried rapping as loud as he could on the glass but without any results. Frustrated, he jogged back to the front in time to see a San Antonio Police Department patrol car pull up to the curb. He watched as the driver got out, put on his hat, and came toward him.

"Problem, Officer? Is something wrong here?"

Maybe Lee had been hurt or had some crisis and couldn't get to the door.

"Maybe you can tell me. Can I see some identification?"

Branch frowned but pulled out his wallet and waited while the cop looked at his driver's license. Both his face and name were well known in the area.

"That do it?" he asked.

"Sorry, Mr. Colby." The cop handed his wallet back. "We got a call from one of the neighbors that someone was creating a disturbance." The guy actually seemed a little embarrassed. "We have to check these things out. You know?"

"Of course. No problem. I was worried when Miss Sullivan didn't answer her door."

"Maybe you could trying calling her first," the cop suggested. He touched the brim of his hat. "You have a nice day."

Branch waited until the man got into his patrol car and drove off before he climbed back into the SUV. He couldn't keep standing in front of the townhouse shouting and making an ass of himself, or at least more of one than he already was. He tried Lee's cell phone again. Still voice mail. He had a very sick feeling in the pit of his stomach that if he didn't fix this soon it might not be fixable at all.

***

Lee burrowed into her bed, pulling the covers tight to her chin, curling up in a fetal position. She had barely made it home and into her bathroom before heaving the contents of her stomach. She'd sat on the bathroom floor for a long time, shaking, before she could manage to get to her feet and tumble into bed. She hadn't even bothered to remove her clothes. She'd let the office know she wouldn't be back that

afternoon because she was all of a sudden not feeling
well. And wasn't that the damn truth?

Every time she thought of the words she'd heard
at Branch's office, she began shaking again. She was
cold. Freezing. And sick to her very soul. Why had
she been such a fool? Such an idiot? She had trusted
him. Acknowledged to herself that she had real
feelings for him. She should have known better. He
was the very reason why she stayed away from
powerful men. Why she kept her sexual relationships
within the walls of Infinity with maybe an occasional
dip in a vanilla lake with a man who appealed to her
on a temporary basis.

She was who she was. At Infinity, she didn't have
to hide it or lie about it. Branch Colby was the first
man outside the club she had indulged in any BDSM
activities with. She had found it incredibly erotic to
"play" the sub without submitting. She had even
entertained crazy, idiotic thoughts that they could
spice up their sex life with it. Maybe even role play.

She had been stupid and should have known
better. It wasn't as if they'd said the L word to each
other. At least not yet. It was way too early in their
relationship, yet she'd been so sure something was
brewing there. A connection. That they were on their
way to something real. What a fool she'd been. Why
would Branch Colby, who could have any woman on
the planet, come after her, anyway? She should have
known he had an ulterior motive, but even beyond
that she wouldn't have expected humiliation to be his
end game.

What she didn't understand was how Max knew
about Mistress Star. Because of her position with the
mayor, she was extremely careful to keep her public

and private personalities separate. If she ever got her wits together again, she'd do her damndest to find out. If it was a member of Infinity, she'd make sure John Francona knew about it.

Her phone rang again for what seemed like the tenth time since she'd gotten home. She'd shut off her cell. Now she reached over and unplugged the landline on her nightstand. If she ever made it downstairs again, she'd do the same to the one in the kitchen. She hated landlines anyway, and she didn't have a real need for one. First on her list of things to do would be getting it disconnected. Presuming she ever got out of bed again.

Her eyes burned, and her throat ached with unshed tears. She hadn't cried for so long, she wondered if maybe she'd lost her ability. She felt used and degraded and ashamed that she'd been taken in with such ease. It would be a long time before she ever trusted anyone again. Or spent time with a man outside Infinity.

***

"Branch?"

He looked up as Karen rapped on his open door then walked into the room.

"Any luck?"

She shook her head. "Same answer. They keep telling me she's out sick, and they don't know when she'll be back." One corner of her mouth ticked up in a smile. "They seem to be quite desperate without her. There's only so much her assistant can do."

"I imagine so. She's damn good at her job." He raked his fingers through his hair. "Thanks, Karen."

Still she stood in front of his desk, as if debating

whether to say something.

"Something else?" he asked.

"Well, if she's ill, and you say she won't open the door or answer the phone for you, perhaps I could go by. She might be more receptive to me."

She looked at him with kind eyes he feared saw far too much.

"What?" he asked. "I know there's something you're biting back, so spit it out."

"I don't know what happened," she began, "or the exact nature of your relationship with Miss Sullivan, but you might want to give it a little time before you try and see her again. Let things settle, so to speak."

"That sounds good in theory." He blew out a breath. "But I have a feeling all the time in the world isn't going to fix this one. I screwed up big time." He gave her a tired smile. "But thanks for the offer and the advice. I think this might take a miracle."

***

Lee put the finishing touches to a media release and saved it on her computer. She hadn't been able to take more than a week off from work, and, even then, things were in a mess when she returned. The mayor was apoplectic but afraid to yell at her for fear she might walk out. She was doing her best to pick up the loose threads and keep things on track. So when her assistant buzzed to tell her someone was there to see her, her initial reaction was to say she was too busy to see anyone right now.

"He says he's on Mayor Vincent's re-election committee," the girl told her, "and he has something he needs to run by you."

Well, hell. This was the part of the job she hated the most, dancing around the politics of it all.

She sighed. "Okay, send him on in, but be sure to tell him, as nice as possible, that I don't have more than a few minutes to spare. Tell him I'll set up a longer time to meet next week."

She was studying her calendar when the door opened and closed and a man's voice said, "I won't take up much of your time."

She'd heard that voice before. At public events and more recently at Branch's office.

Branch! The thought of his name sent shards of pain lancing through her.

She looked up to see Max Ferlita standing in front of her desk.

"Good, because, for you, I have less than a minute."

He held up his hands. "I'll be as quick as I can. I wouldn't be here except I'm on an errand of mercy."

"Ha." She sneered. "If it's on behalf of Branch, he doesn't deserve any mercy."

"You're right. But, Lee? This is as much my fault as his."

She wrinkled her forehead. "How do you figure that?"

"Branch and I have been friends since we were in high school together. We've done a lot of stupid things together. Making bets is one of them."

"Making bets isn't stupid," she snapped, "under the right circumstances. Humiliating people is."

"You're right. I take full responsibility for initiating this one. He was rocked by you at the picnic and wanted to ask you out. And stunned when I told him you were Mistress Star."

She glared at him. "How would you know that anyway?"

"Lee, Branch and I both have memberships at Ultra. We have both been practicing Doms for years. I'm sure you've at least figured that out about him by now. Anyway, I had a guest pass to Infinity one night and saw you there."

Lee dug her nails into her palms to keep her temper under control.

"You know you aren't supposed to disclose information outside the walls of a club without the person's permission."

"You're absolutely right." He nodded. "My bad. I was spouting off to my best friend like the asshole I am, and the thing snowballed."

She wanted to smack him. Spouting off? Snowballed? Did he realize what damage he'd done?

"I'm sure you both had a good laugh when he regaled you with all the details."

"Truth be told, I didn't get any details, Lee. All he said was he lost the bet. He paid me off. A check to the charity of my choice."

"What?" Surprise shocked her. "What did you just say?"

"That he told me he lost the bet, and he wasn't about to divulge any personal details of his relationship with you." He shook his head. "He's miserable, Lee. I've never seen him like this. All he does is work. He won't even stay in one place very long. I'm going to go out on a limb here and say his feelings for you run very deep, and he's not good at verbalizing them. But, of course, to find out, you'd have to agree to see him first."

She shook her head. "I don't know, Max. This has

been—really bad."

"I agree. But if you could please think about giving him another chance. This has been a painful lesson for him to learn."

"Are you sure he never told you anything?" she asked.

"Swear to god. So will you think about it?"

"Yes. But I won't promise anything."

"Good enough. Thanks for taking the time to listen to me."

After he was gone, Lee sat at her desk for a long time, staring at the computer screen and seeing nothing. Could she get past this? See Branch again? Test what they had? She was always going to be Mistress Star, and if he was a Dom—

Still, role reversals had worked for a few couples she knew where both were Dominants.

If she just didn't miss him so much. Not even the pain and embarrassment had been able to wipe that away.

She dropped her head into her hands. Why did her life have to be so complicated?

Chapter Eight

If John Francona hadn't called her and told her
he had a very special sub who had personally
requested her, Lee would still be sitting at home
watching bad movies and drinking hot chocolate and
feeling sorry for herself. John, however, had been
very persuasive.

"You've been absent for far too long, Mistress
Star," he cajoled. "And I have a guest coming in who
has been specific in requesting someone of your
talents."

"Did he ask for me by name?" Was it someone
one of her subs had recommended her to?

"He did. I believe Drew was the one who told
him about you." His voice softened. "Lee, come in for
the evening. I don't know what's causing you to hide
yourself away, but it's time to come out and play
again."

She sighed. He was right. She couldn't stay holed
up in her house every night for the rest of her life. So
now here she was, in her trademark red bustier and
thong and her thigh-high boots with the skyscraper
heels. John greeted her as she came into the lounge.

"Nice to see you again, Mistress Star. We've missed you."

"Yes, well." She let out a slow breath. "I've had some, shall we say, challenges in my life."

"Then I hope tonight will be able to help you deal with them." He lifted a key card from his pocket and handed it to her. "Your sub is ready for you, and waiting."

She raised her eyebrows. "No meet and greet in the lounge first? That's unusual. What if I choose not to have a session with him? What if he doesn't appeal to me?"

John gave her a mysterious smile. "Then you are free to refuse. But I think you'll be very pleased with this one."

"Very well. I guess I can trust you on this."

"Enjoy your evening." He moved aside to let her proceed down the hallway.

Her fingers shook with a slight tremor as she inserted the key card in the slot. When she opened the door, soft music was already filling the air. An aroma lamp dispensed lavender mist in one corner, and all the lights in the room had been dimmed. Except for the spotlights that shone on the board where she'd played with Drew.

Except it wasn't Drew displayed there, immobilized with all the leather straps, skin gleaming with her favorite oil. Instead, she was shocked to see Branch, dark eyes staring at her, watching her. And, for the first time since she'd met him, she saw a hint of uncertainty in his gaze.

For a moment she was tempted to leave, give John back the card, and tell him she'd return when he was through playing tricks on her. Her curiosity made her draw closer to Branch.

"How did you get them to let you in here? What are you doing here? What do you want?"

His eyes never left her face. "I drove the owner of Ultra nuts until he called John Francona to get me a guest pass. I've been waiting for you, hoping we can pick up where we left off. Or start all over, or whatever you want."

Suspicion gripped her. "If this is some kind of trick—"

"No tricks." He chuffed a hoarse laugh. "Believe me, this is not a familiar situation for me. I asked John what things pleased you and whether he would set this up for me. There isn't another woman in the world I'd let myself be trussed up like a turkey for."

She looked at his cock, thick and swollen and protruding between the straps over his thighs and groin. She couldn't stop her smile. "It appears some part of you is happy to see me."

"All of me is happy to see you." He took in a deep breath and let it out in a slow exhale. "Max told me he went to see you. I want you to know I had nothing to do with that."

She nodded. "I didn't think so."

"When he told me he didn't believe he made any headway with you, I was desperate. And desperate people do desperate things."

She wet her lips. "Why didn't you just forget about me, move on to someone else?"

His gaze burned into her. "I don't want anyone else, Lee. It took me a while to admit it to myself, probably because I'm such a stubborn ass. I don't know how to put my feelings for you into words. I've spent too many years conditioning myself not to. But

I want to try to make a life with you. I want us to be together in a permanent relationship."

She narrowed her eyes. A few days ago, those words would have meant everything to her. Now she wasn't sure she could trust them.

"Lee." Branch's voice was hoarse with emotions far greater than pure sexual need. "Listen to me. I know we have challenges here, with both of us needing control. Other couples have made the same situation work. I also know the last night we were together I gave you pleasure. You enjoyed it as much as I did. Please don't deny it."

She couldn't, so she kept silent.

"I think we could build a solid relationship. We can create our own version of a power exchange. I want you to know I'm willing to submit to anything you choose to do with me or to me. That's how much you mean to me."

"Anything?" she asked.

Inside, her emotions were bubbling like liquid in a hot cauldron.

"Anything," he repeated.

As if the word acted as some kind of release lever, everything inside her burst forth, all the anguish, all the pain, all the misery and humiliation. She lifted the short crop on the table next to the board, ready to punish him for what he'd done and how he'd made her feel. Except he hadn't asked for punishment. He had told her without hesitation he was giving her control. That was a privilege, and she would not abuse it. So punishment, no, but pleasure, yes. Definitely yes. Tonight she would be the one controlling his level of desire, taking him on the same erotic journey he'd created for her. Letting her gaze roam his body for a moment, she began striking him with the crop, an instrument whose use she had perfected. With measured rhythmic strokes, she wielded the crop everywhere, all the places experience had taught her would create the maximum stimulation—his shins, his thighs, his arms, his chest. She struck the exposed skin as well as the leather straps, knowing the impact was made more intense by the bindings. She raised and lowered her arm over and over again while Branch lay there not saying a word.

The message in his eyes was *Tonight I am here to serve your needs.*

Her needs. That was what this was. More than eroticism, though, this was a craving on her part to strip everything else from her system. Then she could admit to herself how much she wanted him and cared for him.

Loved him.

Loved him? Was that even possible? Could she give so much of herself to someone? It seemed that was exactly what had happened without her allowing herself to acknowledge it. The hurt, the shame and humiliation she'd felt were so intense because of the swirl of emotions where he was concerned. Could she admit it out loud?

Exhausted, she tossed the crop to the side, tears running down her cheeks with the monumental release of emotions.

"I hated you," she told him.

"With good reason." He had to be in pain, but his voice was steady. Even.

"I never wanted to see you again."

"I know. I was willing to do anything to change

that. I want to be with you, Lee. Forever."

And that undid her. Frantic with need, she began unfastening all the bindings, letting them dangle from the board. When all the restraints had been released, he lifted his arms to her.

"Come here, Mistress Star. Let me hold you."

She shook her head. "I need to attend to your body first. Please let me."

He would have argued with her, but she knew he saw the determination on her face. She opened the package of lotion-infused wipes from the little table and eased one over his body, beginning with his collarbone. When one was used up, she yanked out another until she had soothed his entire body. He never took his eyes from her, and, when she finished, he lifted his arms again.

"Now come here and let me hold you. Let me press you to my heart."

Tears still filling her eyes, she straddled him and pressed herself against his chest. His arms came around her, solid and strong, and she felt the steady beat of his heart.

"I will never be a submissive," she told him, even as she rubbed her cheek against his.

"Understood." He nodded. "As long as you also understand I never will be, either."

She gave a wordless nod.

"But you enjoy the games as much as I do," he continued. "As I will. As we both will. Together."

"And what happens when that need to control becomes more than one of us can handle?" she persisted.

"We'll work it out. We'll set our own rules and adjust them as we go along. Lee, sweetheart, there are many couples who schedule sessions here or at Ultra with someone other than their partner. Let's deal with one thing at a time." He brushed his knuckles across her cheek. "The important thing is we are together. Permanently."

"Can we make it work?" she whispered. "Are you sure?"

"I've seldom been more sure of anything." He swallowed. "I've never told a woman I loved her. I'm not even sure now I know what it means. But what I feel for you is an emotion so huge I can't even give a name to it. Please, please believe me."

Intense emotion choked her. For him to admit his feelings like this to her was huge. Could she do any less? Could she take that step, putting her trust in him? Believe he'd never betray her again?

Yes, the voice inside her head whispered. *Don't lose out on this.*

"I-I feel the same," she whispered. "I had given up believing I'd ever find anything close to what we have, and I don't want to lose it."

"Maybe we'll make our own bets to double down on," he teased.

Then, his expression serious, he threaded his fingers through her hair, drew her face close to his, and took her mouth in a kiss more tender than anything she'd ever experienced. It wasn't demanding. Rather, it was a sharing, a giving, and she gave it right back to him.

When he sucked in an involuntary breath, she suddenly realized the rough texture of her bustier was abrading the welts left by the crop on his body and tried to push herself away.

"Don't move." His arms tightened around her.

"I know I'm hurting you," she protested. "Those bruises are painful." She looked away. "I meant them to be."

He cupped her chin and tilted her head so she was forced to look directly at him. Deep emotion burned in his eyes. "You can attend to my bruises by climbing on my cock. Get rid of that contraption you're wearing so I can feel your breasts on me. Strip off that thong so I can slide into your pussy, which even now I can feel is wet and waiting for me."

He ran his thumb along her jawline. "And no, I'm not demanding. Or even ordering." He brushed his mouth over hers. "Please do it. For me. For us." He managed a wink. "And leave the boots. They're hot."

She literally ripped away the garments, tossed them to the floor, and climbed on him, lowering herself onto his cock. He was right. She was more than ready for him, so wet he glided right into place.

"Ride me, Mistress Star," he told her in a hoarse whisper. "You will always be Mistress Star to me. Let me be your only Dom."

Those words unlocked the last tiny chain around her heart. Ride him she did, slow at first then faster and faster, his large hands holding her in place, steadying her. As aroused as they were, it was scant moments before the orgasm gripped them. They clung to each other as they rode out the storm, shudders racking them, the harsh sound of their breathing ripping through the air.

At last his thick shaft stopped pulsing, her walls stopped spasming, and, breathless, they were still. He held her tight to him, stroking her back with his warm hands. Their journey together would be fraught with pitfalls, but silently they acknowledged they could take the trip together. The prize, the love they would share and a life together, would be more than worth it.

About the Author

Known the world over as the oldest living author of erotic romance, and referred to by *USA Today* as the Nora Roberts of erotic romance, Desiree is three times a finalist for an EPIC E-Book Award (and a winner in 2014), a nominee for a *Romantic Times* Reviewers Choice Award, winner of the first 5 Heart Sweetheart of the Year Award at The Romance Studio as well as twice a CAPA Award winner for best BDSM book of the year, and winner of the Holt Medallion for Excellence in Romance Literature. She has been featured on *CBS Sunday Morning* and in *The Village Voice, The Daily Beast, USA Today, The (London) Daily Mail, The New Delhi Times* and numerous other national and international publications.

Desiree Holt is the most amazing erotica author of our time and each story is more fulfilling then the last. ~ Romance Junkies

Also by Desiree Holt

Joy Ride
Aftershock
Night Mission
He Came Upon a Midnight Clear
Flyover
Lust Becomes You
Overnight Sensation
Soul Dreams
Dark Secrets
Knockin' Boots
Hard Lovin'
Playing with Fire
Wolf Moon
Venus Moon
Blood Moon
Sexy Designs

www.ingramcontent.com/pod-product-compliance
Lightning Source LLC
Chambersburg PA
CBHW072030170626
46811CB00008B/3020